D0432463

Praise for *Anarchy and Old Dogs*

'This is Cotterill's best book, with witty dialogue and engaging characters, especially the irrepressible Siri, who becomes more lovable with each appearance. The combination of humour, social commentary and a clever mystery make this one of the most enjoyable books I've read all year'
Sunday Telegraph

'There is something wonderfully refreshing about the rough-and-ready policing described in Colin Cotterill's addictive series ... Cotterill is a consistently funny writer, bringing a light touch even to scenes of violence and chunks of historical exposition but there is a dark edge to his humour'
Daily Telegraph

'The prose once again sparkles with witty gems and at times makes you laugh out loud at the absurdities of life that Siri so gleefully and matter-of-factly pulls apart. The story moves quickly and grips you tight, as any great crime novel should. Cracking stuff' *Buzz*

'Quercus is the crime publisher to watch ... What Colin Cotterill has mastered, like his Quercus list-mate Adrian Hyland, is putting himself in the mind of a completely different person ... Colin Cotterill has a website worth visiting, but he does not say if he has ever met a Dr Siri in real life. Discovering him now in fiction, I think the author might well have done so in the flesh. Don't leave it too long before you meet him too' shotsmag

Praise for *The Coroner's Lunch*

'Richer plots than Alexander McCall Smith's detective stories, but the same comic charm' *Sunday Times*

'A wonderfully fresh and exotic mystery' *New York Times*

'The story is good, the characters interesting, the hero delightful and the setting fascinating: a find' *Literary Review*

'*The Coroner's Lunch* has been likened to the Botswanan series of books by Alexander McCall Smith, but I would say it is, on the evidence of this first instalment, vastly better' Euro Crime

'Siri's greatest assets are his charm, persistence and dry humour, qualities that also make Cotterill's first novel an unexpected pleasure ... it portrays a credible fictitious world that is vivid and beguiling ... A refreshing antidote to hi-tech crime busting' *Guardian*

'Colin Cotterill's witty novel sharply captures the confusion after the revolution, and its hero, at turns cynical and humane, is an absolute diamond'
Daily Telegraph

'An exotic mix of superstition, ineptitude, and corruption – makes a refreshing change from the usual forensic investigation' *Sunday Telegraph*

Praise for *Thirty-Three Teeth*

'Cotterill's description of this exotic, troubled country is fascinating, and his light touch makes Siri, with his humanity and strange dreams, a very appealing character ... With its endearing cast of characters and some nifty plotting, *Thirty-Three Teeth* is occasionally surreal but always charming' *Guardian*

'Fascinating background, engaging characters and witty dialogue' *Sunday Telegraph*

'Colin Cotterill shows in *Thirty-Three Teeth* that his engaging investigator Dr Siri Paiboun, an elderly coroner with shamanic gifts, should be much better known' *Sunday Times*

'A pleasantly mystical atmosphere that jives nicely with the tropical humidity emanating off the pages' *Time Out*

'The characters are as endearing, and the exotic setting as interesting, as in the first episode' Jessica Mann, *Literary Review*

'[Siri] has Sherlock's logic, Quincy's forensic skills and Rumpole's ability to stick to the letter of the law, when expedient so to do. What makes Cotterill more than just a clone of previous experiments is the attention to detail, history and language ... It's a quick, easy read, which ... makes you want the next one sooner' *Scotland on Sunday*

'Triumphantly braves the tightrope between quirky humour and the surreal macabre ... magically sublime' *Entertainment Weekly*

Praise for *Disco for the Departed*

'Witty, elegant and informative' *The Times*

'[A] joyfully inventive mystery series ... Cotterill's plots are dense but his characters supply ample reward' *Sunday Business Post*

'Delightful ... the merit of these stories is their wit and their droll way of poking fun at a corrupt, inefficient bureaucratic communist administration ... the book is remarkable again for its very unusual locale but mainly for satire, wit and good humour' Tangled Web

CURSE OF THE POGO STICK

Colin Cotterill

Quercus

First published in Great Britain in 2009 by Quercus

Quercus
21 Bloomsbury Square
London
WC1A 2NS

A CIP catalogue record for this book is available from the British Library

ISBN 978 1 84724 809 1 (HB)
ISBN 978 1 84724 817 6 (TPB)

10 9 8 7 6 5 4 3 2 1

Printed and bound in Great Britain by Clays Ltd, St Ives plc

This book is dedicated to the Hmong and other hill tribes-people of Laos who fought reluctantly on both sides of the political battlefield. I am sad for the betrayals they've suffered in their lives. I hope I haven't represented them inaccurately in this book, and I thank all those who helped with my research. I apologize for any liberties I may have taken to give my book more cheer and hope than real life has afforded the Hmong. Apologies also to missionaries Dr G. Lynwood Barney and William A. Smalley for using my own transcription and trashing their fine Hmong phonetic system – but it gave me a headache.

FORM A223-79Q

ATTENTION: Judge Haeng Somboun
C/O: Department of Justice,
People's Democratic Republic of Laos

FROM: Dr Siri Paiboun

RE: National Coroner

DATE: 13/6/1976

RESUME:

1904 Plus or minus a year - years didn't have such clear boundaries in those days. Born in Khamuan Province, purportedly to Hmong parents. I don't recall it myself.

1908 Whisked off to live with a wicked aunt.

1914 Dumped in a temple in Savanaketh and left to the will of the Lord Buddha.

1920 Graduate from the temple high school. No great feat.

1921 Buddha investment pays off: shipped to Paris by kindly French sponsor intent on making something of me. The French make me start high school all over again just to prove it wasn't a fluke the first time.

1928 Enrol at Ancienne Medical School.

1931 Meet and marry Bouasawan in Paris and join the Communist Party for a lark.

1934 Begin internship at Hotel Dieu Hospital. Decide I might want to become a doctor after all.

1939 Return to Laos.

1940 Frolic in the jungles of Laos and Vietnam. Reassemble broken soldiers and avoid bombs.

1975 Come to Vientiane hoping for a peaceful retirement.

1976 Kidnapped by the Party and appointed national coroner. (I often weep at the thought of the great honour bestowed upon me.)

Sincerely,

Dr Siri Paiboun

CONTENTS

PROLOGUE

As there were no longer any records, the Hmong could not even tell when they actually misplaced their history. The event had deleted itself. But the oral legend that was passed on unreliably like a whisper from China would have them believe the following:

The elders of the Hmong tribes had gathered to lead the great exodus. For countless centuries, their people had been victimized by the mandarins. With no more will to fight, the time had come to flee. Traditional nomads, the Hmong had few valuable possessions to carry. They would lead their animals and build new homes when they reached the promised lands to the south. But there was one artefact that belonged to all the Hmong. It was the sacred scroll that contained their written language, legends, and myths of ancestors in a sunless, ice-covered land, and, most importantly, the map of how to reach their nirvana: the Land of the Dead in the Otherworld.

With great ceremony, the scroll was removed from its hiding place, wrapped in goat hide, and given the position of honour at the head of the caravan. The Hmong walked for a hundred days and a hundred nights and on the hundred and first night they were lashed by a monsoon that drenched them all before they could find shelter. Cold and wet, they sat shivering in a cave until the sun rose. The keeper of the scroll was distraught to discover that the rain had soaked through the goat hide and dampened the sacred document. Chanting the appropriate mantras, they unrolled the text and laid it on the grass to dry beneath the hot morning sun. And the followers, exhausted from their sleepless night, found shade under the trees and fell into a deep sleep.

While they slumbered, a herd of cattle found its way up to the mountain pass and discovered both the sleeping Hmong and the hemp scroll inscribed with vegetable dyes. And, starved of new culinary experiences, they set about eating this delicious breakfast with vigour. The Hmong awoke to find their sacred scroll chewed to pieces. They chased off the cattle and collected the surviving segments. These they entrusted to a shaman who stayed awake with them and kept them safe and dry for the next hundred days and hundred nights. But on the hundred and first day, the clouds finally parted and the sun shone and the Hmong found themselves in a deserted village. Not one to ignore the lessons of experience, the shaman laid out the segments in the loft of the longhouse. Certain the remnants of the scroll wouldn't be attacked by cattle or goats or birds there, he finally joined his brothers and sisters in a well-earned sleep. But he hadn't taken the rats into account. Half-starved and desperate, the rats set about the hemp and devoured it in a frenzy. Unsated, but with the memory of food now implanted in their minds, they then turned upon one another. When the Hmong finally climbed into the loft, all they found were several ratty corpses and a few unreadable shreds of their culture. This, according to the legend, was how the Hmong lost their history and their written language.

The spirit of the first-ever Hmong shaman, See Yee, looked up from the Otherworld and was mightily pissed that his people could be so careless. He stewed over this for a lifetime or two before he could find it in his heart to forgive them. But he didn't send them a new scroll or a new script, for that really would have been tempting fate. Instead, he taught six earthly brothers how to play six music pipes of different lengths. By playing together, this sextet found they were able to guide the dead to the Otherworld without the map. But, as they got older and found themselves with more personal commitments, it wasn't always easy to get them together to perform. So See Yee taught mankind how to put the six pipes together and play them with six fingers as one instrument. Thus, the *geng* was born.

When the *geng* was played, people swore they could hear the voices of the ancestors. It was as if their spirits were retelling the history and describing the path to the afterlife through the sounds of the instrument. Music became the medium through which the Hmong recorded their legends. The notes had replaced the written text. The music of the *geng* could be used to teach new generations about their past and their future lives. They had no need for books.

The Western missionaries, of course, had no ear for such foolishness. They considered a race without a written text to be barbaric and ignorant. So, they created a roman phonetic system as the basis for a script for the Hmong that was impossible to read without learning a lot of complicated rules. The clever churchmen believed they had bonded together the diffuse Hmong tribes through this linguistic subjugation, but the Hmong knew better. They learned the text to keep the missionaries in their place, but they had a system that was far more advanced than anything devised in the West. They had a musical language that communicated directly from one soul to another.

1

THE STIFF

'What is that god-awful row?'

'One of those Hmong beggars playing his flute by the sounds of it.'

'Well, it's annoying. Doesn't he know this is a hospital? Can't you go tell him to shut up?'

'You've got legs. You tell him.'

'I'm in the middle of something.'

'And I'm not?'

The morgue was made of concrete, and secrets had no cracks to hide in. From their corpse-side seats, Nurse Dtui and Madame Daeng could hear every disparaging word the two clerks spoke. The auditors were like an unhappily married couple. The pale-faced men in their frayed white shirts and polyester slacks had ghosted in the previous morning. They'd handed Dtui their official placement papers from the Justice Department and commandeered the office. They'd taken advantage of the coroner's absence and chosen this week to go through his books for the 1977 audit. It appeared they'd been instructed to find errors in the records. Dtui had known straight away that that task was virtually impossible, given that her boss had handwriting so horrible he could hardly read it himself. Dipping a cockroach in ink and having it scamper around the page would have left more legible traces to the average reader.

But Nurse Dtui had to admire the auditors' determination. They had every flat surface in the office covered in a layer of grey papers and were tiptoeing barefoot between them. They'd been through the entire first drawer of the filing cabinet and were making copious notes in their ledgers. They'd been instructed not to discuss their mission with menial staff so Dtui had no way of helping them find whatever it was they were searching for.

'Let's go and get lunch,' one of them said.

'Hm.'

It was the first thing they'd agreed on since their arrival. Dtui and Daeng heard one or two paper rustles, the closing and locking of a door that hadn't been squeezed into its misshapen frame for many years, and a cough from just outside the room where the two ladies sat.

'Can I help you?' Dtui asked.

'Comrade Bounhee and I are taking our lunch break,' said one of the men.

'Perhaps you'd like to come in here and join us for a sandwich?' she suggested. Daeng smiled and shook her head. The men hadn't dared enter the examination room since the arrival of the corpse that morning.

'Er, no. Rather not. Good health, comrade.' And he was gone.

There were four rooms of a sort in the only morgue in the People's Democratic Republic of Laos. The paper-strewn and off-limits office was one. Then there was a large alcove and the cramped storeroom in which Mr Geung, the lab technician, stood polishing specimen jars. And finally there was the examination area they all referred to as the cutting room. It was here that Nurse Dtui and Madame Daeng sat on either side of the deceased military officer, finishing their tea. Despite appearances, there was nothing perverse in this irreverent act. It had been necessitated by the peculiar events of that morning.

Mr Geung had a form of Down syndrome that made him very efficient at repetitive tasks and very thorough in those duties he'd been taught. Anything out of the ordinary, however, caused him to become flustered. He didn't trust strange people or equipment that disturbed the norm in his domain. The auditors had been such an intrusion and he continued to mutter his displeasure to himself. But there had been one other annoyance that week. The morgue's perfectly good French refrigeration unit had been replaced with a Soviet behemoth twice its size. Neither the hospital engineer who installed it nor Mr Geung, who was responsible for turning it off and on, had any idea how it worked. Dtui could read Russian but none of the dials seemed to perform the functions they promised. So Mr Geung had been particularly distraught to discover that after only two hours in the unit the army captain was deep frozen.

Madame Daeng, the coroner's fiancée, had arrived just then to discover Dtui comforting a teary Geung, and a large ice pole of a corpse on the tray. It was made all the worse by the fact that an unknown surgeon would be coming to conduct the autopsy that afternoon in the company of Mr Suk, the hospital director. The body had to be thawed out somehow before their arrival. They agreed that wrapping him in blankets would only have the effect of preserving the frozen state. It was a comparatively cool early December day and there was no heater. Madame Daeng, always calm in a crisis, suggested they wheel the soldier into the sunlight that filtered through the louvred window and sit close to the body so their own body heat might warm him up. The only other heat producer they could find was the Romanian water-boiling element. They plugged it in, placed the water pot at the end of the stainless-steel dolly, and watched it bubble.

As there was water on the boil and margarine peanut biscuits in the tin, why not, they thought, have a cup of tea or two? For modesty's sake, and to catch the crumbs, a white cloth was draped over the captain's nether regions. And there they sat, discussing the latest items to have disappeared from the shops.

'How's he doing?' Daeng asked.

Dtui poked the skin with her spoon. 'Another hour and he should be ready.'

'And who's performing the autopsy? I thought Siri was the only one in the country qualified.'

'Well' – Dtui leaned back in her chair – 'technically, Dr Siri isn't all that qualified either. I mean, he's good, but he doesn't have any formal training as a coroner. Our politburo didn't seem to think that fact was terribly important; surgeon – coroner, same difference. Luckily for them, Siri's a bit of a genius in a number of ways.' As Dtui wasn't sure how much Daeng knew about the doctor's spirit connections, she kept her praise vague.

'So, today . . . ?'

'Is some young hotshot surgeon who just got back from East Germany. He went over there as a medic six years ago. Amazing what they can achieve in the Eastern Bloc. Must be some type of fast track. But the new boy isn't qualified to perform autopsies either. If our friend here hadn't been a soldier they'd probably have kept him on ice till Siri got back. But the military are really curious to find out what killed their officer. The boys who brought him in said he hasn't even been identified yet. They're waiting for his unit to report him missing. The hospital director asked Hotshot if he could do an autopsy in a hurry and the fellow evidently said, "How hard can it be?" Well, we'll see.'

'It would have been a lot harder if we hadn't thawed him out. I think it must be working. I'm starting to get a whiff.'

'Me too.'

'It looks like we generate more body heat than we thought.'

It was true. Both women had good reason to glow. Big, beautiful Dtui could thank her first sexual experience for the baby taking shape inside her. Fortunately, Phosy the policeman had done the right thing. Auntie Bpoo the fortune-teller had said the child would be a girl. Their daughter was barely three months along and Dtui had already given her a name and started to crochet pink sun hats for her. She would be fat and jolly and intelligent like her mother . . . and she'd be a doctor . . . and she'd get married before she got pregnant and not at a registry the week after the test came back positive. In that respect she wouldn't be like her mother at all.

Madame Daeng glowed because, at sixty-six years of age, she'd been proposed to by a man she'd secretly loved for much of her life. When she had been reunited with Siri in the south just a few months earlier, those same old girlish feelings had still gurgled around inside her. She and Siri were both widowed now – both battered by cruel circumstances in a country that had only ever known war. But the two old warriors were gloriously open to new love. She'd unashamedly followed him back to Vientiane and kept her fingers crossed. Siri had proposed to her in a most un-Lao fashion: with flowers. To her joy he'd acquired that peculiar habit during his years in France. She'd refused him, of course. What respectable woman would accept a man's first offer? And, luckily, he'd asked again, over coffee, not a flower in sight, and this time she'd accepted. They would marry immediately upon his return from the north.

'Do you suppose we can leave our little soldier now?' she asked Dtui.

'Absolutely! Let's go open your restaurant. If he thaws out any more he'll insist on coming with us.'

Mr Geung agreed to watch the body and the two glowing ladies climbed onto their respective bicycles and rode out of the Mahosot Hospital grounds. They tinkled their bells as they turned left on Mahosot Road even though there was very little chance of being hit by anything but other bicycles. Vientiane was a cyclist's paradise. Unless they had friends in the Party, very few citizens could afford to fill up their motorcycle tanks with petrol. Cars had become house-front ornaments. The sound of a passing engine prompted little children to run to the street's edge and wave. Siri might have been right. Laos *was* shrinking back into a preindustrial age.

Dtui and Daeng rode past peeling signs that pointed to services and establishments that had ceased to exist, past long-since vacated spirit houses and leaning telegraph poles that seemed to be held up by the wires strung between them. The few tarred roads were frayed at the edges like nibbled licorice and the sidewalks were clogged with unkempt patches of grass. They pedalled along the Mekhong past Chantabouli Temple to the little noodle shop Daeng had acquired on her arrival in the city. It wasn't a particularly bright period to be setting up a new business. But she'd brought with her a reputation as a cordon bleu noodleist. The word had spread and even though it was only eleven thirty, hungry customers were already gathered in front of her shuttered store. When she arrived they cheered and made bawdy comments. Humour was one of the few glues that held people together in hard times.

'Been visiting with your gynaecological nurse, have you, Madame Daeng?' one asked. 'I suppose you'll be making an announcement sometime soon.'

'If I were to make that particular announcement you could expect to see the world press gathered out here,' she said. 'Now, move aside and stop your insolence.'

Dtui and the customers helped her open up and move some of the tables out to the street side. They wheeled the portable kitchen to the front of the shop and Daeng lit the twigs and charcoal to get the water boiling. She'd prepared all the ingredients before heading off to the morgue; now she only needed to parboil the noodles. While they were waiting, she poured everyone a cup of cold jasmine tea. At last, Dtui and Daeng stood side by side at the stand dishing out *feu* noodles in deep bowls. When the better part of the crowd was fed, Daeng leaned toward her friend.

'So, are you going to tell me what's bothering you?' she asked.

'What's that, auntie?'

'Something's crawled into your head since we left the hospital.'

'Oh, I don't know . . .'

'Tell me.'

'It's the body. There's something wrong with it.'

'What?'

'I don't know. I'm just getting one of those feelings. It's like when Dr Siri tells me I'm looking but I'm not seeing. Or perhaps I'm seeing but I'm not getting it. Oh, listen to me. I'm just trying to be clever like him. I wish he was here, you know?'

'Me too.'

They were there, trespassing in the private grounds of his snooze. They loitered – those malevolent spirits – like teenage thugs, never in focus but there nevertheless. Wherever his afternoon siesta led Dr Siri Paiboun – down forested paths, through bombed towns – they lurked and watched him pass. He was aware of them in every dream. The *Phibob*, the ghosts of the forest, had no more useful occupation than to hang about in his subconscious and remind him of the constant threat they posed.

Dr Siri was the reluctant host of Yeh Ming, a thousand-year-old shaman. During that old witch doctor's comparatively short stay on earth and his comparatively long sojourn in the afterlife, Yeh Ming had caused no end of grief to the dark spirits and now they sought revenge. 'A load of old supernatural pig swill,' some might say, and two years earlier Siri would have been the loudest in the chorus. But now there was not a doubt – no question. Only the charmed stone amulet he wore around his neck hung between Dr Siri and a nasty end.

Although he hadn't yet mastered his unwanted life, he'd learned to live it. Despite all this occult thuggery, the old doctor purred in his sleep like a snowy-haired cat. His chin rested on his chest and a barely audible snore resonated through his nostrils. At seventy-three years of age, he'd learned how to sleep through all variety of meetings and conferences undetected. He hadn't once fallen off his seat. Of course, he was built for balance – short and solid – and from the distance of the speakers' platform he appeared to be just one more rapt member of the thousand-plus audience, deep in thought. In truth, only the extreme volume of the Vietnamese loudspeakers could have drowned out the collective buzz of hundreds of snoozing cadres. If the generator had failed that chilly afternoon, residents of Xiang Khouang would have gone running to their homes in fear of a plague of bumblebees.

Most of the regional delegates had been up through the night slurping sweet rice whisky through bamboo straws and reminiscing with long-lost allies. Siri, more than most, had endured the thanks of countless old soldiers he'd repaired in battlefront surgery. He'd accepted a glass from each of them and was ill-prepared for seven more hours of keynote addresses and reports. It would have been impossible to withstand such torture without the odd nap or two.

It was around three when he regained consciousness in time to learn that 'The quintessential socialist is patriotic, technically and managerially competent, morally upright and selflessly devoted to the greater social good,' but he'd forgotten to bring his notepad. He caught sight of his boss, Judge Haeng, nodding enthusiastically in the second row. Siri clicked the bones in his neck and instinctively reached up to scratch the lobe of his left ear. He'd lost it in an altercation a few months before but its spirit continued to tingle. Damned annoying it was. He shifted his weight from buttock to buttock to revitalize his circulation and looked absently around him. The regional representatives sat unfidgeting like maize on a breezeless day, silently counting down the minutes. Although Stalin had never actually bothered to write it down, Siri was aware that a good communist had to be a good Buddhist. Only meditation and a banishment of pain could get one through a day of Party political bull.

Siri looked with admiration along the furrows. Only one undisciplined cadre had succumbed indiscreetly to fatigue. He sat two rows in front, six seats across. Obviously the quarterly Party Planning and Progress Conference had been too much for him. He slumped like a wet rag in his chair, his head hanging uncomfortably backward, staring at the temporary tarpaulin roof. One would have to be extremely tired to adopt such a drastic pose – or dead as an absent earlobe. Siri opted for the latter. He calmly stood, pushed past knees to the end of his row and more knees to the seat of the dead comrade. The disturbance in an, until now, unruffled event caused the speaker on stage to lose his place in his speech and look out at the mêlée.

Siri, delighted to have an opportunity to make something happen on this otherwise wasted day, felt for a pulse in the old cadre's neck and shouted with unhidden glee, 'This conference has suffered its first fatality. There will undoubtedly be more.'

2

HOW TO BLOW UP A CORONER

In Vientiane, the autopsy of the unknown soldier began four hours late due to the fact that socialism had somehow made time more flexible. There were often situations when 1:00 PM and 5:00 PM were interchangeable. Director Suk and Surgeon Mot got to the morgue at exactly the time everyone was supposed to be on their way home. The director had been diverted to supervise the placement of a flower bed – the hospital's first – courtesy of the Vietnamese Elderly Widows Union. A regiment of dazzling yellow chrysanthemums stood guard in the centre of the compound. This event had coincided with the arrival of the first batch of nurses trained in Bulgaria. Naturally Suk had to appear in several photographs with the nurses and the flowers and sign endless documents related to both distractions. The doctor had found himself in an unscheduled political lunchtime seminar that dragged on through the afternoon when no consensus could be arrived at with regard to the collectivization of bean farming.

The only good news resulting from this delay was that by now the captain was completely de-iced. Then there was the fact that Dtui had been given four more hours to look at the body and the uniform it had arrived in. It had allowed her time to confirm in her own mind that something was very wrong. She wasn't absolutely sure what that was, but she was confident enough in her instinct to know that the autopsy could not go ahead.

She was standing by the corpse feeling below the soldier's rib cage when Surgeon Mot marched in.

'Nurse!' he said. 'What exactly do you think you're doing?' He was skinny as a drip of rain down a window with hair like a poorly fitting Beatles wig. He had a large bloated nose and saggy eye bags. Dtui's first impression was that Surgeon Mot had suffered in East Germany. To compensate for his suffering he'd adopted an inappropriate German arrogance. Dtui could see nothing Lao in him.

'Dr Mot,' she began.

'Nurse, step back, please.'

'But, comrade . . .'

'Did you not hear me?'

At that moment, Director Suk walked into the cutting room and took up a position as far away from the corpse as possible. There was no secret at the hospital that the man hadn't a stomach for medical matters. He was an administrator. He was followed close behind by a gentleman in uniform whom nobody bothered to introduce. Dtui guessed he was a military observer although the insignia on his uniform was faded from overwashing and he wore white socks that peeked over his boots.

With an unnecessary flourish, Mot pulled back the towel that lay across the lap of the corpse. Dtui grew more anxious. She appealed directly to Suk.

'Director! I strongly recommend you postpone this autopsy.'

'Oh, I see,' said Suk with the usual sarcastic smirk. 'Dr

Siri goes away and his nurse takes over the administration of the morgue. Is that the way we run things here?'

Mot reached for the large scalpel and left Dtui with no choice. She stepped across him and grabbed his skinny wrist. She knew if it came to a fistfight she could take Mot but might have trouble with all three of them.

'What the . . . ?' Mot was shocked.

'Nurse Dtui,' Suk shouted. 'What on earth has come over you?'

'This body,' she said. 'I think . . .'

'Well?'

'I think it might be booby-trapped.'

There were a few seconds of stunned silence before the three outsiders burst into laughter. Mot squirmed his hand free from the nurse's grasp.

'It looks like somebody's been sniffing the formaldehyde,' he laughed.

Unnoticed, Mr Geung slipped into the storeroom, leaving Dtui without an ally.

'I'm serious,' she said. 'Look there. You're a doctor. What do you see at the side of his abdomen?'

'Do you suppose we could tell her to leave?' Mot pleaded. 'I didn't undergo six years of training by experts to come home and be lectured by a country girl. This job is difficult enough as it is.'

Dtui was red faced with anger.

'I agree entirely,' said Suk. 'I apologize. Nurse, kindly leave. I'll see you in my office in the morni—'

But his train of thought was derailed by the sight of Mr Geung emerging from the storeroom with an AK-47. It was pointed directly at the new surgeon, who fell backwards against a chest of drawers.

'Y . . . you c . . . can't laugh at Comrade Dt . . . Dt . . . ui,' Geung said. 'Ih . . . ih . . . it isn't nice at all.'

'Now, son,' Suk said, as if talking to a wild beast, 'calm down. Don't do anything . . .'

Geung swung the AK47 in his direction and the director flattened himself against the wall like a layer of paint. Only the soldier remained passive. There might even have been a slight glimmer of a smile on his lips.

'Let the nurse say what she has to say,' he suggested.

'Well, thank you,' Dtui said, one wary eyebrow cocked in Mr Geung's direction. 'What a girl has to do to get a word in these days.' She smoothed down her white uniform, which strained at the buttons when she pushed forward her ample chest.

'Dr Mot,' she said. 'I'm sorry to have to do it like this but, well, you just wouldn't listen and it might very well be a matter of life and death. Admittedly it might also be a false alarm but no harm in being careful, I say. Don't you agree?'

The gun swung back towards him and he nodded enthusiastically.

'Good, then perhaps you could tell us what you see there at the side of the abdomen.'

The surgeon stepped up to the body. 'Of course, it's a wound.'

'Excellent. And what type of a wound is it?'

'Apparently a new one. The stitches haven't yet been removed.'

'Right. Now take a closer look at that wound, would you?'

He leaned over it. 'But it's just a regu— Oh, my. That's odd.'

'What is?' the soldier asked.

'There's been no healing, there's no scar tissue at all.'

'And that means?'

'That this incision was made post-mortem,' Dtui cut in.

'Why would anyone want to open a corpse and sew it up again?' asked the soldier.

'Exactly. And there's something else,' she said. 'Feel this, Doctor.'

She gently guided the surgeon's hand to a point just below the rib cage. 'Don't press too hard now.'

The doctor ran his finger back and forth.

'It feels like some kind of protrusion. A broken bone? No, it's too narrow.'

'There's one exactly the same on the other side,' she told him.

'Really? How peculiar.'

'My guess,' Dtui said, 'is that something was put inside this fellow's stomach after he died.'

'Whatever for?' Suk asked, scraping himself from the wall.

'If it's a practical joke,' Dtui said, 'it's a very elaborate, even a *sick*, one. The only logical explanation I can see is that someone's sent us an exploding corpse.'

'Oh, I say,' said Mot, taking a step back. 'Who would do such a thing?'

'Someone who doesn't like coroners,' Dtui guessed. 'Or, more specifically, someone who isn't fond of Dr Siri. I'd guess they didn't know he'd be off partying in the north.'

The soldier pushed past Geung and stepped up to the table. 'If she's right, your nurse here might just have saved our lives.'

'*If* she's right,' said Suk with one eye on the AK-47. 'It sounds pretty far-fetched to me.'

'There's something else,' Dtui continued. The captain's uniform jacket was hung over the back of a chair. She held it up and poked her finger through a small hole in the back. 'Do you know any officers in peacetime who'd knowingly wear a jacket with a bullet hole in the back? There isn't a corresponding hole in our corpse so I know it isn't his.'

'You're right,' said the soldier. 'No commanding officer would let him walk around with a hole in his jacket. He might not even be military at all. Someone could have dressed up this body in an old army uniform.'

'Why?' Suk asked.

'Because they knew there wouldn't be an autopsy otherwise,' Dtui supposed. 'But if the corpse is a dead soldier, they knew we'd insist on one. What do you say, Doctor?'

Mot shook his head in bewilderment.

'I'd say nurses have come a long way since I went off to the Eastern Bloc.'

'We still can't be certain,' Suk said. 'We have to confirm this booby-trap theory or we'll all look like fools. Look, can't you get this idiot to put down his weapon?'

'It's just a decoration, Director,' the soldier said. 'No moving parts, I'd bet.'

'Well spotted,' Dtui laughed. 'It was a prop in the Red Ballet. They came to give us a show last month and left it behind. Our Mr Geung wouldn't have dared pick it up if it was real. He doesn't have a violent bone in his body, do you, love?'

Geung smiled his gap-toothed grin and offered the stage prop to the director, who waved it away angrily.

'As for the bomb theory,' she continued. 'We can't be certain how sensitive it is. I suggest we carefully put him back in the freezer and ice him again. Once he's good and hard we could pop him over to the X-ray Department and see what we're dealing with.'

'Excellent idea,' said the soldier. 'And in the meantime I'll get in touch with our bomb-disposal people and have them standing by just in case. Very well done, lass. Very well done.'

It was almost midnight before everything was sorted out. It transpired that Dtui's hunch had been spot-on. There was nothing subtle about the device in the captain's stomach cavity. It consisted of a spring steel hacksaw blade bent around and fastened with fishing line like a very taut bow. Halfway down the bow was a hand grenade whose pin was attached by a second wire to the opposite side of the blade. The entire stomach sack had been removed, presumably to prevent leaking stomach acid from dissolving the wire prematurely. The device was placed in such a way as to leave the tips of the bow pressed against the abdomen wall. A normal Y incision as performed by even the most incompetent of coroners would have sliced through the fishing line. The bow would have sprung apart, thus removing both the pin from the grenade and the presiding pathologist from life on earth. Dr Mot, Director Suk, Geung, and the unnamed soldier undoubtedly owed Dtui their lives.

Madame Daeng could only laugh when she discovered they'd been taking tea beside a booby-trapped corpse. Her reaction surprised Dtui no more than the old lady suggesting they warm up the body together in the first place. She'd been a resistance fighter, a saboteur, probably an assassin. What was one little bomb in one more dead body to Madame Daeng? Now troubled by arthritis and forced to wear glasses to read, she described herself as 'just another old biddy'.

But there was no missing the spark in her eye or the fire on her tongue. No white cotton-wool perm for her. She wore her hair short and wild. Had there been an ocean and a navy to sail it in Laos, she'd have outdrunk every man. And she knew stories that would make a monk's toenails fall out.

Dtui had liked Daeng from the moment she'd laid eyes on her and, given their admiration for the same man, it was inevitable they'd end up best friends. Unlike most Lao, Dtui wasn't one to respect the elderly per se, but she found herself deferring to the old lady. It was Saturday and the lunchtime rush had subsided. They sat at a table at the front of the shop eating boiled peanuts and watching the herons surf the breezes above the Mekhong. It occurred to those who took in the view with a cynical eye that the far bank was getting farther away. In the two years since the communists had taken over Laos, the river had become a sea, their tiny country, an island. In the first year people had abandoned her for fear of political persecution. Now they were taking their chances crossing the river because they couldn't feed their children. *Pasason Lao* newspaper that week had rather smugly announced that the per capita income had soared to ninety American dollars per annum. It didn't mention that one in four children didn't make it to the age of five. The people across the border in the refugee camps ate better. Dtui had briefly tasted that freedom but she was Lao down to her roots and for better or worse – mostly worse – she loved her country.

Like notes on a bar of music, a flock of birds had come to perch on the telegraph wires opposite. Daeng had been attempting to hum the tune they wrote. She gave up and looked at her friend.

'Is anybody investigating it?' she asked.

'As much as they're able. Half the Vientiane police force is up in Xiang Khouang protecting the delegates at the conference.'

'Including your adorable husband.'

'They might have to bring Phosy back. It was an assassination attempt against government employees. That's right up his alley. The army doesn't want to have anything to do with the story any more. Once they realized the corpse wasn't military they pulled out. It's a civil case now and the regular witless wonders of the constabulary are on it. Some teenager in his big brother's uniform came to interview us this morning. He had me fill out a crime questionnaire. I wasn't supposed to talk about anything that wasn't mentioned on the form. Can you believe it?'

Daeng swept the empty peanut shells into a hill on the tabletop.

'So, in reality, until Phosy gets back there is nobody investigating.'

'Right.'

'Then I don't suppose anyone would object . . .'

'. . . if we asked a few questions of our own? Shouldn't think so. Where do you think we should start?'

'I suggest we make a list of people who might want to see Siri dead. Anyone he's antagonized recently.'

'A list like that would include half of the politburo, but I doubt they'd go so far as to blow him up. Although I'm not so certain about his boss, Judge Haeng.'

3

A FATE WORSE THAN DEATH

'Do you really think it was necessary to yell it out at the top of your voice, Siri?'

Judge Haeng, head of the Justice Department and perennial thorn in Dr Siri's backside, had the old surgeon cornered.

'I could hardly imagine my voice would carry all the way to the platform, considering it was an open-air meeting hall.' Siri smiled serenely.

'Well, it did. And I could see the angry expression on the chairman's face quite clearly. You sometimes forget you represent the Justice Ministry at these events.'

'Really? I thought that was your job.'

Haeng clenched his fists. Although he would have preferred it otherwise, he was the coroner's superior. He was a young man with a boyish, pimply face and an iffy Soviet education. Upon his return from the Eastern Bloc, despite his lack of experience, character, and personality, the Justice staff had kowtowed and given him the impression he was worthy of the position. Only one, Dr Siri Paiboun, had stood up for himself. Their run-ins had been frequent and the score in terms of victories overwhelmingly favoured the doctor. The Justice Department had needed a coroner, and Siri, despite his indifference to the position, was the nearest to one the country had. It was a Lao-Mexican standoff. Haeng couldn't fire Siri and they both knew it. But in its own ironic way, the conflict had become one of the perks of the job for Siri.

'You know what I mean, Dr Siri,' Haeng said. 'A disobedient child in school reflects poorly on the upbringing by his father.'

Siri chuckled at the inappropriateness of the analogy, making Haeng even angrier.

'And what would you have me do?' Siri inquired. 'Leave the poor chap there secreting his final bodily fluids all over the seat?'

'Surely . . . surely you could have been more discreet?'

'You mean whispered for the people in his row to pass the body down to the end?'

'Just think in future, won't you? Of course we'll need an autopsy.'

'An autopsy? He died of boredom. You won't find traces of that anywhere on the dissecting table.'

'Don't be ridiculous. A long-term Party member dies mysteriously at a national conference. It's our duty. The politburo would expect nothing less. My decision's final.'

'Ah, so it's a show. Should we sell tickets?'

'It is not a show. It's a decent, responsible socialist act. His family will be grateful.'

'They'll die of embarrassment when they find out.'

But Haeng was no longer listening.

'Oh, and one more thing.' Siri's big bushy eyebrows rose like synchronized caterpillars to the top of his forehead. 'We won't be flying back to Vientiane on Monday.'

'Why not?'

'The prime minister wants the Justice Department to

show its confidence in security measures in Xiang Khouang. The province has a history of unrest and we need to let them know we support their efforts to keep down the scattered resistance. The PM has suggested we drive to Luang Prabang.'

'Oh, good God.'

'I suppose you have a problem with that also?'

'Why me? I'm a coroner. What confidence will that instill?'

'I admit I didn't want you along, but I think today's little exhibition booked you a place. I imagine the senior members believe it would . . .'

'Teach me a lesson.'

'You bring it upon yourself.'

'But driving? I hope they'll give us enough sticky rice and raw fish to last us a month.'

'I'm assured the road has been cleared and the bridges repaired all the way through. It's the dry season, Siri. We could be in Luang Prabang in a day or two.'

'And the president's wife might grow a penis on her chin.'

'Don't be vulgar.'

'I hope we're going in a tank. Unless it's been rerouted, that road passes directly through enemy-controlled territory. Aren't you afraid of getting shot?'

Although the judge paled, he managed to keep his chest out in front of him.

'Where have you been, Siri? Don't you read the *Khaosan* newsletters? There is no enemy. He's been vanquished. All we have now are one or two Hmong rebel gangs hiding in the jungle. Even so, we'll be travelling with crack People's Liberation Army commandos. It'll be safer than crossing Lan Xang Avenue. Don't be afraid, old fellow.'

Siri wasn't afraid. He was devastated. He knew the road was awful. Even in a tank they wouldn't arrive in under a week. And, as for vanquishing the enemy, that was far easier in an editorial in *Khaosan* than in real life.

The Hmong had first migrated to Laos from China almost two centuries before. They were a people forced through their swidden – slash and burn farming – lifestyle to move on every five to ten years when the fields became unproductive. Originally, land had been plentiful and this was no problem. But soon, with overcrowding on the plains, they were forced to higher and higher ground. They were a race with no nation, no large cities, and few ambitions beyond family and home. They lived according to tradition with the elders teaching everything technical, moral, and spiritual to the young. But history constantly found them in the wrong place at the wrong time. Opium cultivation had been imposed on them by the Chinese and French administrators, then they were taxed for producing it. When they supplied to the wrong side, they were hounded off the land. They found themselves in a system they'd had no desire to enter, constantly having to fight for their independence. When they fought it was not out of conviction but for their own survival.

In Laos, interclan rivalry was exploited at the time of the Japanese occupation. One clan collaborated with the Japanese, the other with the French. This split became even more pronounced after the war, with one side forming an alliance with the communists in the north and the other with the Americans. There was very little option of nonalignment. The Lao Hmong lived in a land that had forever been somebody's battleground. Diverse groups who had no interest in politics were forced by their clan name to favour one side or the other. Clans found themselves pulled into the fray by recruiters. Once again, the Hmong had become somebody's enemy – a title their culture abhorred and, given their history of abuse, one they hardly deserved.

Once rallied, the Hmong were fierce fighters and all those who battled alongside or against them vouched for their valour. It wasn't until 1973 that a cease fire was called in the protracted civil war but the suffering hadn't stopped for the hill tribes. In 1975, the so-called thirty-year Hmong who had sided with the Pathet Lao were somehow forgotten when the communists took control of the country. There were token positions and ranks allocated, but the majority were either sent back to grow opium, or, worse still, relocated to the plains, where they succumbed to diseases unknown in the mountains.

The Hmong who fought with the CIA under General Vang Pao were also forgotten by their allies. The Americans could retreat to the land of the free and the brave, but the Hmong had nowhere to go. They were the enemy in their own land. They weren't extended the luxury of being ignored or relocated. They were hunted. They fled, of course, some to the camps in Thailand, other old soldiers to the mountains around Phu Bia, where they formed the *armée clandestine* in a hopeless resistance against the PL. Others still formed bandit gangs and vented their frustration on their own kind. Once again, war had divided a culture, split families, and left only shells of the proud men and women who had fought and lived to tell the tale.

No, it wasn't the Hmong Siri was afraid of. He'd been in battles all his life and survived. A bullet to the head wouldn't have been that much of an upheaval to him now. What distressed him was the thought of being stuck in the jungle with spotty-faced Judge Haeng for a month. That, he decided, would be a slow and agonizing way to go.

There wasn't a lot for individuals to do on a Sunday in Vientiane. At least from Monday to Saturday a person could work for next to no pay and spend her evenings doing community service for the sheer joy of it. But Daeng was officially a business proprietor and Dtui had recently moved to her new husband's rooms at the police compound so neither was registered for the Sunday community development programmes. This meant there wasn't even a slim hope of clearing garbage from the banks of the irrigation ditch or laying gravel on a dirt road while singing 'The Blood We Shed for the Republic Has Turned to Sweat.'

So, instead, they rode their bicycles to the little metal bridge at kilometre 2 that crossed over to Don Chan.

The river island was man-made, the Mekhong having been diverted into an aqueduct to supply water for the city long before the establishment of the Nam Ngum waterworks. In the rainy season nothing more than a humble stub poked from the water, but now the island and its sandbar stretched way back past the city. Small holders and farmers had rebuilt their bamboo huts and fresh green vegetables sprouted in abundance. It was the ideal spot for a picnic. Dtui and Daeng's spread consisted of river-fish cakes, sapodilla-flavoured rice wine, and of course, vegetables with still-beating hearts plucked from the earth before them. They sat at the top of an eight-foot-high bank, close enough to Thailand to see their affluent neighbours taking lunch, sitting at tables watching their poor Lao neighbours cross-legged on the grass getting pickled.

'Do you think they wish they were here?' Dtui asked.

With the baby working on its personality inside her, she'd decided this would be her last drinking day. Even so she sipped modestly at the sweet wine. Daeng was a serious drinker and she more than made up for Dtui's abstinence.

'Why not?' Daeng replied. 'I've seen wild birds in the branches of trees looking enviously at caged song doves. We all of us want what we can't have. Do you wish you were there?'

'I was there, briefly. I liked everything about it. It's so modern. The stores have so much choice compared to ours. They're crammed with all kinds of goodies. But . . . I don't know, I wondered where it would end. You get a rice cooker and you lust for an oven. You get an oven and you want a chef to come and cook for you. Once you get into that cycle you can never be satisfied.'

'So, you prefer having nothing.'

'I appreciate things more. And I don't have *nothing*. I have friends. I have a reasonably good life – a socially responsible job – experiences. I mean, how many people get to hang out with a legend of the underground movement?'

'Oh dear. You can't believe everything Siri tells you, you know.'

'Yes I can. He's told me all about you. He says what he believes. That's why I respect him. I wish I had nerve enough to blurt out what I actually feel, like he does.'

'That luxury comes with age. When you're younger, you don't always get away with saying what you believe, particularly in this type of system.'

'Did you think it would end up like this? When you were fighting the French? Did you think the alternative to colonialism would be so . . . so claustrophobic? Did you think we'd be looking over our shoulders all the time worrying we might be doing or saying something to offend the Party?'

'We're in transition, Dtui. Things will get better. At least we Lao are in control of our own destiny now.'

'If you don't count the Vietnamese "advisers".'

'We'll shake them off. Have faith. The worst is behind us. We haven't known real peace for my entire lifetime. Let's sit back and enjoy it while we've got it. By the way, my glass is empty.'

'Yes, Your Highness.'

They lay back in the thick buffalo forehead grass for a while and listened to the slow, soothing motion of the river trickling through the reeds.

'I'm starting to feel guilty,' Dtui confessed.

'How so?'

'I feel like we should be off catching the bomber.'

'I've told you. Patience is a vital component of a successful investigation. Rushing into it without a plan is a waste of human resources.'

'The trip to the police station yesterday was a complete waste of human resources. What did the boy say? "And why should we share our findings with you two . . . ladies?" Talk about insolence.'

'Right. But didn't that inspire us to think laterally? And didn't that period of thought lead to our brilliant insight?'

'Your brilliant insight.'

'It was our idea.'

'I remember exactly how it went. You said, "If you were the assassin, Dtui, what would be going through your mind on the day of the bombing?" And I said I'd want to make sure my bomb actually went off and did its damage, seeing as there'd be no chance of its making the evening agricultural broadcast on the wireless. And you said, "That means the bomber would have to be on the hospital grounds that afternoon."'

'It was the only way he could be sure.'

'And you said, "Perhaps we could ask the staff whether they noticed anyone hanging around all afternoon on Friday."'

'Right, but it was you who remembered the nurses and the photographs. It wouldn't have entered my head.'

'Yes it would. And it probably won't help anyway. When the prints come back from the shop tomorrow all we'll see is smiling nurses and flowers. Not a bomber in sight. He's hardly likely to pose with them, is he now?'

'So little faith in one so young. Remember, anything's possible.'

'There must be more we can do. If only we could get access to the army bomb squad report or the police investigations. I'm sure we could do more than the boy wonders.'

'Until Siri and Phosy come back it's just you and me. I have all kinds of contacts in high places in the south but nobody up here – not yet.'

Dtui poured Daeng another shot from the misty bottle and filled her own glass with water. They toasted the diners across the river.

'I do,' Dtui said.

'Do what?'

'Have an influential friend. You do too. Or at least an ex-influential friend.'

'You don't mean Civilai?'

'I certainly do.'

'Oh, Dtui. He's retired.'

'Cronyism doesn't just go away overnight.'

'He isn't going to be in any state to help us.'

Daeng knew of several other reasons why the ex-politburo member would be reluctant to help them. A few months earlier, Siri had uncovered a plot to overthrow the Lao government. Dtui and Phosy had crossed over to a refugee camp in Thailand to spy on the deposed Royalists. Information they gleaned there had led to the failure of the coup. But in the aftermath, Siri had discovered that his old friend, Civilai, was in line to take a post in the proposed revolutionary administration. He was a traitor, a fact that only Siri and Daeng were privy to. Civilai had taken early retirement in return for their silence. Daeng doubted the old politician would be prepared to step back into the quicksand from which he'd so recently escaped.

Dtui knew none of this. 'Let's find out,' she said.

In the words of Comrade Civilai, the rainy season of '77 had been as brief and unconvincing as a politician's credibility . . . and he should know. Since his strongly encouraged retirement from the politburo three months earlier, officially for health reasons, he'd had a lot of free time to perfect his witticisms. His best friend, Dr Siri, had been afraid the traumatic events leading up to the old man's fall from grace might have driven him to despair and an early visit to the pyre. But far from it. Civilai had expanded in all directions like a man released from the grip of atmospheric pressure. His mind had been given rein to consider philosophies beyond Marx and Lenin. He'd begun to listen to the lyrics of his grandniece's pop music and see merit in them. He'd started reading the novels hidden in his loft and breathing in their beauty. Not since his French education had his mind been so liberated.

His body too had expanded. His skin no longer stuck to his bones like pie crust. Always a food connoisseur, Civilai now had endless hours to engage in his passion. He delighted in his wife's cooking and experimented with his own. He invited friends for dinners, performing miracles with the scant offerings on sale at the morning market and the Party co-op. He had, they all agreed, blossomed and bloated as a result of his divorce from politics.

Dtui and Daeng sat with him at the round kitchen table in a house that had once belonged to the director of the American high school at kilometre 6. It was what the English would call a bungalow and what the Lao would call a rather pointless style of architecture – not raised from the ground on stilts to allow the air to circulate and the floods to pass beneath. Windows of glass that magnified the rays of the sun. A toilet with a communal seat that encouraged the exchange of germs and disease. But the senior Party members didn't live there because it was practical. They'd moved into the walled US compound to thumb their socialist noses at the Americans. They'd endured and survived the endless air raids on their cave enclaves in the north-east for thirty years. The enemy owed them.

Daeng was pleased to see how well the old comrade was looking. Only she and Siri knew the actual reason for his retirement and both had sworn not to discuss it again. Dtui, like the rest of Laos, saw him as an elder statesman in frail health who had retired gracefully. But there was nothing frail about him on this day.

'I must say it's rare that I get two voluptuous lady visitors at the same time,' he said. 'Nice to see I haven't lost that magnetism. How did you get here?'

'On our bicycles,' Dtui told him.

'All this way? And you with your arthritis, Madame Daeng.'

'Can't let a little chronic pain spoil a day out, comrade,' she told him.

'That's the spirit. Then I think you both deserve a drink for making it here.'

'I'm on the baby wagon, uncle,' Dtui confessed. 'But Madame Daeng got quite sloshed at lunchtime. I think that's why she can't feel her legs.'

'Nice to see,' said Civilai, pulling down several bottles from the Formica wall cabinet. 'Then she'll need topping up.'

'Where's Madame Nong today?' Dtui asked, wondering whether Civilai's wife would let him tipple in the afternoon if she were around.

'Women's Union excursion . . . again. She's been signing up for all of them since I became redundant. Can't really understand it. You'd think she'd want to spend all her time cleaning up after me, wouldn't you?'

'You'd think so.' Daeng smiled. 'We girls are mysterious creatures.'

'No arguments from me there.' Civilai nodded, arriving at the table with three full glasses with lime slices hanging onto them for dear life. 'So, what can I do for you, ladies?'

They sat and drank their vodka sodas – one without vodka, two with little soda – while Dtui told Civilai all about the peculiar happenings at the morgue and the reluctance of the police and the army to share their findings. He agreed that, although there were several dozen people who might like to give Siri a good slapping, none that he could think of disliked the doctor enough to blow him up. He recalled one attempt on the coroner's life a year before but as far as he knew there had been nothing personal about it and the perpetrator was safely behind bars.

'When's Siri due back? Civilai asked.

'Tomorrow evening,' Dtui told him.

'Then we'd better get cracking. We can't have our chief and only coroner killed by some maniac, can we now?'

'You think you can help?' Dtui asked.

'Undoubtedly. If a respected Party dinosaur can't call in a favour or two, who the blazes can?'

Some people just die. Siri had come to that conclusion after many years of careful observation. They don't necessarily die *of* anything, they just get old, everything gives up, and they pass away. It's as simple as that. There are those who describe it as dying of old age but that puts old age in the same category as bubonic plague and the Black Death. There really is nothing dangerous about old age and there's no reason to be afraid of it. It certainly hadn't done Dr Siri any harm. He'd been passing through its hallowed halls for some years and it hadn't killed him.

Comrade Singsai had passed away in his sleep during an excruciatingly long speech discussing the allocation of cattle. It was rather sad that his last memory on earth might have been how to encourage bulls to increase their semen count. But he was old and he'd endured a full life. He hadn't been able to summon the energy to pull himself out of a pleasant dream and back into that never-ending conference. Who could blame him? Siri was sorely tempted to write 'He just died' on the death certificate but he knew that wouldn't satisfy anyone. He'd invited Haeng and a couple of the other seniors to observe the autopsy, and, as he expected, they'd declined.

Siri was surrounded by five-litre cans of exotic fruits from China, crates of vegetables, stacks of packs of processed meat, sacks of rice, large bottles of soft drink syrup, tins of sardines and pilchards and a whole wall of goods labelled in Russian that could have been anything. There was enough to feed a medium-sized town for a year. And tucked at the back of the potatoes were several pallets of Vietnamese 33 beer in dusty bottles. In the arsenal of most coroners is a piece of equipment known as a skull chisel. It's primarily used to separate the calvarium from the lower skull but it has a useful secondary purpose in that it opens beer bottles very well. Siri looked at his watch, popped a 33, and made himself comfortable on the rice sacks.

From somewhere beyond the formality of the Party gathering, the mystical sounds of a *geng* pipe drifted across the plain. He'd heard it before on the grounds of Mahosot before leaving Vientiane. He let the music seep into the pores of his skin and smiled at familiar phrases and intimate passages. It was a magical, heavenly refrain that felt out of place in such a godless spot.

The decision to hold the national conference in the old city of Xiang Khouang had been pure showmanship. After a prolonged period of Royalist-American bombing, the only structures still standing were one house, a broken hospital wing, and a twenty-foot Buddha with half a head and shrapnel wounds. There was nowhere to eat or sleep or even to hold a conference in the devastated place. But the Lao People's Revolutionary Party had a point to make regardless of the inconvenience to the participants. The stage and a thousand chairs and countless tarpaulins had been trucked down from Phonsavan, the new provincial capital. And there in the centre of the main street they gave their speeches and clapped and let the defeated enemy know who was in charge. All around them in the pockmarked landscape, several thousand tons of unexploded ordnance lay hidden beneath the dried mud. Leisurely strolling during the breaks was strongly discouraged. For the same reason there were no sightseeing tours arranged to the Plain of Jars. Instead, each participant had been given a colour postcard of a buffalo beside an ancient four-foot pot in his orientation folder.

At the end of each day, the delegates had been bused back to Phonsavan to eat and sleep in preparation for the next day's ordeal. And it was in a dining hall storeroom that Siri now sat. An hour and two more beers after his arrival he'd hidden the empty bottles behind a stack of mandarin oranges and gone to the door with his bag. Judge Haeng and two officials were seated at a table in the dining room.

'It's done,' Siri said and he laid the death certificate in front of the judge. It read 'cardiac arrest'.

'See, Siri?' Haeng said. 'See? That wasn't so difficult, was it?'

'Judge Haeng,' Siri nodded, 'you're right again. Oh, by the way, I redressed him for collection.'

Siri was sure the officials would order one or two labourers to remove the cadaver. Nobody would think to check under the shirt. Comrade Singsai would return to his family with his body and his dignity intact.

'Oh, Siri,' Haeng called after him as he headed out into the evening chill. 'Get to bed. We're off early in the morning.'

Siri's response wasn't audible, which was perhaps just as well.

4

EXPOSED NURSES

The hospital had allowed the new nurses ten exposures on the official Mahosot camera. It was a Brownie, a souvenir of the American days when money was available and the stores had been stocked with medicines and equipment. But now, as Director Suk made perfectly clear, the camera was not for recreational purposes. It was for recording medical achievements (of which there had been none to date), documenting autopsies, and recording historical events. The arrival of the first batch of nursing students to return from Bulgaria was technically a historic event so the girls had been given permission to use up the remaining exposures on the film as long as they also captured the chrysanthemums.

Dtui accompanied the nursing cadre when she went to pick up the photographs from the pharmacy behind the evening market. Developing photos had become something of a sideline for the pharmacist since film was hard to come by and so few people had moments to celebrate. He'd made copies of the Mahosot pictures for each of the eight nurses. But one of the young ladies had been so impressed by the facilities at the country's leading hospital, she'd fled the dormitory and was last seen floating across the Mekhong holding onto an inflatable neck brace. That left one set of photos for Dtui.

With the office still inhabited by auditors, Dtui and Daeng spread the pictures across the dissecting table.

'Where do we start?' Dtui asked.

'Well, anyone with binoculars and a false moustache,' Daeng said. 'If that fails we'll settle for someone who looks out of place.'

That objective was simplified by the fact that seven of the ten photos were exclusively of seven smiling nurses, one unsmiling nurse, and a flower bed.

'I don't suppose the nurse who absconded had anything to do with it, do you?' Dtui asked.

'I imagine there are easier ways to get into the hospital grounds than spending four years in Sofia, but we won't rule it out.'

'Right!'

One of the remaining three snaps was a very good picture of the morgue itself with nurses pointing to the sign and one young thing pretending to be in the throes of a horrible death. That left only two with people in the background. One, of the nurses walking across the grounds, contained a handful of patients who had been shooed from the wards to enjoy the therapeutic rays of the sun. They all looked convincingly ill. Only the last shot offered any hope. It was what is known in photographic terminology as a mistake. In the foreground was an out-of-focus breast and an arm, but in the background was a panorama of three hospital buildings with several dozen people standing and seated and walking about. They were far too small to identify. Neither Daeng's reading glasses nor the base of a petri dish could magnify them to any recognizable size.

'Damn,' said Dtui.

'Patience,' said Daeng. 'We'll find a way to enlarge them.'

*

On the map provided by the Xiang Khouang constabulary, the road to Luang Prabang was a distinct red line. It began in the old capital of Muang Khun and headed north-west through Phonsavan, the replacement capital, which was still not entirely built. It proceeded past the Plain of Jars before wriggling its way west to Luang Prabang. And, indeed, the journey to just beyond the Phonsavan intersection was comparatively smooth and untroubled. The convoy consisted of two armoured vehicles, two Land Rovers, and one open jeep crammed with armed guards. Its composition belied the theory that there was no longer an enemy to be afraid of.

The first Land Rover contained the deputy head of the National Police Coordinating Committee, his Vietnamese adviser, and Comrade Colonel Phat, the adviser from Hanoi attached to the Justice Department, or, more specifically, attached to Judge Haeng. Since the signing of the Treaty of Cooperation and Friendship in July, there was hardly a department head who didn't sport his own Vietnamese minder like an unwanted hump. The judge himself had opted to ride in the second Land Rover with Siri and a bodyguard. This was not an indication of his growing fondness for the coroner but rather an escape from more unwanted advice. Siri had offered to travel in the jeep with the soldiers but Haeng reminded him of how inappropriate that would be for a man of his standing. Siri pointed out that socialism had removed class barriers but the judge threw an axiom into the ring for which there was no rhyme or reason or riposte: 'The yellow-headed cornsucker bird can be starved and beaten and spun around a hundred times and transported a thousand miles but still its innate instinct will lead it home to a familiar land. In the same way, the common man will always know where he belongs.'

With that bafflingly cruel aphorism still in his head, Siri had cornered Phosy, his favourite policeman and surrogate son-in-law. He'd begged the officer to accompany him on the trek.

'I need a human being to talk to,' he'd pleaded. But Phosy was assigned to bigger cheeses than Dr Siri and there was nothing he could do about it. Siri was on his own.

Despite the fact that their mission was supposed to instill confidence in the beleaguered law enforcement officers of Xiang Khouang, the only professional stop they made that first day was at a little police box in Ban Latngon. The officer wasn't in attendance but they knew he couldn't be far because his uniform and underwear were drying on a string line beside it. As they sat waiting for his return, Siri could hear the secret language of the *geng* wafting down from the hills. And some of the sounds were taking on the form of words to him. He was certain he heard the name of his inner shaman, Yeh Ming, and something about a young girl and a demon. But the words were often lost in the notes like a puzzle and when he looked around at the other members of his party, it occurred to him he was the only one paying attention to the music. He wondered whether anyone else could even hear it.

After half an hour they gave up on the errant policeman and left him a note before resuming their journey. As Siri had feared, Haeng wasn't the type of passenger who sits staring idly at the passing scenery. He'd had many years of experience of pummelling people into submission with his points of view. Along the way he'd memorized a thousand Party slogans and made up a thousand more. He was the type who never asked a question that warranted more than a yes or no reply, so when they first stopped to shoot rabbits – the polite man's euphemism for having a wee – Siri had found himself a painful lip bush. The leaves were spongy and surprisingly sound resistant. He'd used them during the war to block out the headache of constant mortar fire. He assumed that if they were able to deaden the percussion of battle they should be more than adequate to erase the inane chatter of Judge Haeng. All Siri needed to do was nod or shake his head from time to time and his superior was satisfied.

Cloaked in this new peace, Siri took in the spectacular scenery. He'd lived in it, of course, but in war one never had the luxury of appreciating the beauty of nature. Every hill, every mountain had been a threat then. But in the slow-moving convoy that took them through Latngon and further west toward Kasong, he had the time and space to enjoy his splendid country. Every turn in the road revealed a new calendar photograph. The mountains rose from misty valleys like Chinese watercolours. It was the land of birds, of jungle sounds, and of lushly delicious vegetation. He was delighted that the fighting hadn't destroyed it all. Thankfully, Mother Nature always managed to find a way of repairing man's abuse of her. And no more than twelve kilometres from Ban Kasong she even began to stamp her authority.

The rains had long since ceased in the north-east but the road had yet to recover from them. The ruts in the dirt track they called a highway were deep and crested as if a choppy sea had been carved out of dry mud. In places there was nothing flat to drive on at all. The soldiers in the lead car would jump from their vehicle with spades and attempt to level a way through the clay breakers. They were barely thirty kilometres from Phonsavan when the captain in charge – the setting sun already turning him into a silhouette – summoned the men to pitch their tents and call it a day.

Siri unplugged the leaves from his ears and smiled at Judge Haeng.

'Not bad,' he said. 'Thirty kilometres already. At this rate you'll be my age by the time we get to Luang Prabang.'

'Yes, Doctor?' said Haeng. 'And where will that leave you?'

'In a far better place, Judge.'

In the jungles of Xiang Khouang there were wild tigers, Malay bears, and wolves. Very few of them lusted for human flesh but the ominous night chorus they broadcast would leave a young city boy with fears for his life. Although Haeng had grown up in the north-east he wasn't the hardy, outdoors type. The son of an affluent Chinese businessman who chose his allies well, Haeng had been a child of the Party, a red scarf-wearing zealot, the type who gladly informed on his schoolmates. While his father was trafficking arms in one direction and opium in the other, Haeng's Lao mother had nurtured in her son a sense of fair play and equality, but as in most privileged upbringings, equality didn't amount to giving away their wealth and sharing what they had with the lower classes. This dichotomy had continued to confuse young Haeng even when his father decided the time was ripe to send his eldest son to study in the Eastern Bloc. A second boy was sent to China and a third to Australia to hedge all bets. One could never tell in which direction the political winds would blow in the region.

Even in Laos the businessman had been canny. Unbeknownst to the Pathet Lao, the astute Chinese had played both sides right up until the cease fire in '73. When it became clear the Royalists were unlikely to triumph, he focused his allegiance and large sums of money on the communists. By then the ideological investment he'd made in his first son was reaping dividends. Haeng was already a senior Party Youth cadre in the Soviet Union and had done well in school. He'd studied law to a level students from the third world were permitted to reach and it seemed plausible the boy would soon be able to return to Laos in some senior management position. But his father wanted more. It took a generous contribution to the Soviet Ministry of Justice to persuade them that an expeditious course in advanced law for Indochinese students would be invaluable to his son. So, in nine months, a second-class law degree that carried no weight in the USSR was upgraded to a judgeship in Laos, which had even less meaning.

While his fellow Party members had lived in caves for a generation, Haeng had managed to completely avoid fighting and roughing it in the jungle. In fact, hard as it might be to believe, he'd lived something of a playboy lifestyle in Moscow. Even in the sixties there was fun to be had in the Soviet Union for the children of the Marxist capitalists. He had lived well there and returned reluctantly to Laos to take over a justice system vacated by the fleeing Royalists. There was no longer a constitution, which meant there were no laws so his role was largely ornamental. Other than trying the odd divorce, frolicking with cheap and easy nightclub singers, and drinking the nights away, he had little to busy himself with.

But there was plenty to occupy his mind on this first

night of their road trip. He lay wide awake in his tent as the light from the fire danced its fingers against the canvas. The ground was hard and lumpy. The air was so cold he could see his breath. And, all around, wild beasts reminded him that he was invading their territory. He hated the prime minister's office for ordering this tour but he knew these were early days in his climb to power. He was an outsider in this bureaucracy of old men and, as such, wasn't particularly trusted by any of them. He had a good deal of favour currying to do before they'd accept him into their inner circle. And one thing Judge Haeng was good at, one might even say virtuoso, was kissing arse.

December in the mountains of Xiang Khouang was too cold and high for mosquitoes. Siri slept in a hammock slung between two sturdy drooping breast-fruit trees. Wrapped in a blanket, he smiled up at the stars that extended from horizon to horizon. They shone brightly like sunlight squeezing in through nail holes in the atmosphere. He breathed in the scents: the night orchids that hid their beauty shyly during the day and blossomed under moonlight, the release sourness plants, and the sudden love vegetables. He listened to the jungle musical: the choir of birds and beasts that sang through the night. The air was so fresh he could feel his insides waking from a long polluted hibernation.

Although not, as they say, in the flesh, the old lady was back. She sat in a most unladylike pose, with her *phasin* skirt above her knees, her arms folded across her chest, and her head nodding from side to side. Her mouth was a clot of unspat betel nut. She was with Siri often these days. She neither spoke nor gestured nor came nor went. She was there and then she wasn't. The monk at Hay Sok Temple had suggested she could have been Siri's mother – or could still be. Tenses were annoyingly unhelpful when it came to the afterlife. As Siri had been separated from his parents at an early age, there was no way to tell one way or the other, and she certainly wasn't giving anything away.

He fluttered his fingers at her. 'Goodnight, Ma,' he said, and closed his eyes.

Dtui sat in the cutting room with nothing to do but admire the smiles of the seven happy nurses and the scowl of the one malcontent in the Mahosot photographs. The auditors in the office had been buoyed by the news that Dr Siri wouldn't be back for another few days. They'd been warned of his reputation and doubted he would welcome their intrusion. It was hard to believe the little morgue had enough paperwork to keep them engrossed but Dtui noted that their snouts were still dipped into the filing cabinets. Mr Geung was using a long-handled broom to sweep away the ceiling cobwebs and the spiders seemed to appreciate his lack of coordination.

'I doubt those spiders have recovered from the laugh you gave them yesterday, brother Geung,' Dtui said.

'A . . . a morgue c . . . can't be too clean,' he told her, quoting Dr Siri.

'You're sweeping all the paint off the walls.'

Geung, with his very personal sense of humour, found that comment hilarious. He almost choked behind his surgical mask. Dtui heard a loud cough from the office that presumably suggested that menial staff shouldn't be having fun on the job. Geung leaned against the table while his friend slapped him between the shoulder blades. When his voice returned, he said, 'I know who sh . . . she is.'

He was looking at the photographs.

'Yes, you do. They're our new nurses,' Dtui reminded him.

'No.' He picked up the photo of the nurses walking across the hospital compound. He pointed – not to the girls but to the patients who sat watching them pass. In particular he singled out one old lady in pyjamas sitting in a wheelchair.

'You know her, do you, pal?' Dtui took a closer look: thin as a noodle strand, white haired, certainly ill.

'No, Dtui. I don't kn . . . know her. I just kn . . . know who she is. And you know t . . . too.'

'Do I?' She looked again. 'Give me a clue.'

'On the the wall of the Bureau de P . . . Poste.'

'The wall of the . . . ? Oh, you aren't thinking it's – what's her face?'

'The Lizard.'

'No way!'

Dtui looked again, shaking her head. The Lizard? Her wanted poster had been on the wall of the post office for several months as a result of the last case Dtui, her husband, Phosy, and Dr Siri had worked on together. According to Security, not only had the Lizard been involved in the last coup attempt, she'd been wanted for ongoing acts of terrorism against the Republic since it came into being. Customers at the Bureau de Poste probably believed the old lady's photo had been attached to the wanted poster as some kind of joke. How could such a sweet old thing be wanted for crimes against the state? But there was nothing funny about the Lizard. She had a chip on her shoulder against the communists and now it seemed that grudge had extended to revenge. But this couldn't be . . .

Dtui brought over a petri dish and looked through it at the old lady in the wheelchair. Old women tended to look a lot alike to Dtui but there was something about the expression in the woman's eyes that made Dtui think Geung had a point. And as that thought took root in her head, a second idea occurred to her. If she was after revenge, what if Siri wasn't the intended victim? Dtui and Phosy had played a key part in putting down the coup. What if the lizard lady knew Siri was away, or didn't care? The ends of Dtui's fingers tingled and a shudder ran down her spine. She looked once more at the old girl in the wheelchair. Geung was right. This was the woman who glared from the shadows of the post office wall.

Their evening meeting couldn't come soon enough.

5

SHOTS FROM THE GRASSY KNOLL

'Because they're basically heathens,' spat Judge Haeng.

Their journey had been painfully slow and the judge's lack of sleep made him more opinionated than ever. The convoy was negotiating one obstacle after another: a river with no bridge, a temporarily filled bomb crater that had reopened, a tree the breadth of a man's height sprawling across the road. They were currently on a track that clung along the edge of a steep incline. The valley below dropped drastically to their left. Luang Prabang seemed half a planet away. As there was no pocket chess or solitaire to while away the nonmoving hours, Siri had removed the plugs from his ears and was having sport with his judge. The driver and the bodyguard were both listening so Haeng was obliged to fight every point.

'Simplicity doesn't necessarily mean barbarianism,' Siri countered.

'Simplicity, Siri? They allow their youth to fornicate before marriage. That isn't simplicity. The Hmong are completely without morals.'

'I think you'll find they have some of the strongest morality taboos of all the ethnic groups.'

'Premarital sex not being among them?'

'I suppose it depends on whether you classify sex as a sin.

There are worse things. I've heard some of our public officials take nightclub singers from such places as the Anou Hotel and have their way with them for money. Is that morality, Judge?'

Siri enjoyed the blush on the young man's cheeks. He knew the Anou was one of the judge's favourite fishing holes.

'Unsubstantiated rumours, Siri . . . about whoever it is. I'm surprised at you, taking notice of market tittle-tattle.' Siri smiled but held back. 'And besides, we're discussing hill tribes. I'm trying to explain how some savage races still have a way to go, not only educationally, but morally and socially.'

'Really? I've heard the Hmong social order is the most disciplined and traditionally ordered of all the minorities. A Hmong's family is his life.'

'Not much of a life to give, is it?'

'Now, now, Judge Haeng. If I didn't know you better I'd say you were talking like a bigot.'

Haeng laughed. 'Doctor, you couldn't be further from the truth. Some of my closest friends are from the backwoods. You do realize how much effort the Party directs at fringe groups?'

'By fringe, I take it you mean the forty per cent of our citizens who aren't native Lao?'

'Exactly. I take it you've read the new draft constitution?'

'I was waiting for the movie version. But I take it you've had a hand in writing it.'

'More like an entire arm, Siri. I'm particularly proud of the passage that reads, "Our pluri-ethnic people will have to intensify their patriotism, become closely knit, eradicate all prejudice and discrimination inherited from the former society, be mutually supportive, and help the disabled so that all efforts may be devoted to the construction of our beloved country."'

'Hmm, you're right. That wasn't at all racist.'

'Did it occur to you we have ethnic schools in every province?'

'Where you teach . . . ?'

'Standards, Siri. We teach standards and discipline and Lao language and history.'

'In schools two weeks' walk from a village, in classrooms where few people speak a familiar language.'

'Of course not every child is able to attend. We have to select the brighter children.'

'Like Hitler.'

Judge Haeng's acne flared like neon from the frustration of teaching new tricks to an old dog. Siri was calmly peeling a mandarin. A silver pheasant flapped in front of the slow-moving vehicle. The driver and Siri smiled at the omen. Haeng didn't notice.

'We need to educate them, Siri. Do you know?'

'Know what, Judge?'

'Know what their religion is?'

'Judaism?'

'Shamanism, Siri. They believe in spirits. They have witch doctors dealing with medical matters.'

There came a distant rumble as if the earth had a stomach complaint. The dry lotus garland that hung from the rear-view mirror began to swing wildly. Haeng seemed oblivious to it.

'They hold séances and exorcisms—'

'Judge Haeng?'

'—and devil worship. What kind of children . . . ?'

The world seemed to fall on them at that moment. The

entire cliff came crashing down in front of the Land Rover. Rocks and earth smashed the windscreen and dented the hood. Siri turned his head in time to see the jeep far back on the road disappear as another wall of rocks and uprooted trees landed between them. He believed it was only a matter of time before a boulder – a big lump of rock with his name engraved on one side – came crashing onto the roof, leaving him and his boss a dimension short, flat and lifeless as roti. He even looked up defiantly at the car's overhead light. But the end didn't come. Only a peculiar silence he felt obliged to break.

'Well,' he said, 'that's livened up an otherwise dull day.'

He promised himself he'd never shout at a Party conference again. He wondered how much more hopeless the situation could become, but he didn't have long to wait for an answer. The first bullet hit a tyre and their vehicle sank toward the north-east. The bodyguard began to fumble at his holster. The second bullet grazed the roof.

'Oh, my God,' Haeng screamed. 'It's an ambush.'

Siri finished peeling his orange and handed a slice to the panicking judge. He knew from experience that all the squealing in the world wouldn't help them now. Bullets whistled in their direction from the steep grassy incline above them. The driver ducked into the space beneath his steering wheel and hugged the foot pedals. The bodyguard finally had his shaking pistol in his hand. His first shot narrowly missed Haeng and smashed the rear window.

Haeng screamed, 'We're surrounded.' He fell across the guard and grabbed for the far door handle. 'Siri, for heaven's sake. Do something.'

Siri ate the orange slice and wondered. In the brief few seconds since the ambush had begun, he'd already come to a conclusion. If the attackers really wanted them dead, the passengers would have been knocking on the gates of Nirvana after the first volley. Over twenty shots had been fired and only the first had made contact. If this wasn't an attack by some blind bandit gang, the ambushers had a plan for them.

'I suggest you relax,' Siri shouted above the gunfire.

'Idiot!' shouted Haeng. It was his last word. He was able to wrestle open the door and, in throwing himself out, he managed to drag the bodyguard with him. Both men tumbled onto the dust and scrambled on all fours into the vegetation below. Within a second they were out of sight. Siri felt a sharp prick at the back of his neck. He turned to see a figure, the head wrapped in a sarong with just a narrow slit for the eyes. They were beautiful eyes. The assailant held up a thin stiletto as if to show Siri what had done the damage. Before he passed out, Siri offered the young lady the remnants of his orange.

'Look! You can't just play policeman,' Phosy told the three amateur sleuths sitting around the table at the back of Madame Daeng's shop. Moths and flying beetles strove to avoid collisions as they circled the hanging lightbulb above their heads. 'Let the professionals handle this, won't you?'

A burst of laughter would have been less bruising to his professional pride than the ironic raised eyebrows and pursed lips that met his comment.

'What?' he asked. 'We have good people.'

'And you are one of them,' Civilai assured him. 'But until your return this afternoon, it appears that the charge sheet had sat in an in-tray on somebody's desk.'

'We're understaffed.'

'And will continue to be,' Civilai added. 'And meanwhile, your pregnant wife is in extreme danger.'

Dtui remained diplomatically silent. Phosy looked around at the unlikely detectives. He'd tried and failed to deter them from irresponsible acts in the past and he had to admit, as a team, they were far more effective than the converted foot soldiers he was training at police headquarters.

'Well, I suppose attack is the best form of defence,' he conceded. The group cheered. Dtui gave his cheek a friendly sniff and refilled the glasses.

'Good,' Madame Daeng said. 'So, let's get down to it. Comrade Civilai, what other insights did your contacts come up with?'

'The military believe the hand grenade in the stomach of the corpse was one commonly used by the Royal Thai Army. As most of the aggression against us is launched from that side of the border, I suppose that's only to be expected. As we only identified the Lizard from the photograph this afternoon we haven't had time to contact the department at the Security Division responsible for her case file.'

'I can do that,' Phosy told them.

'And we're certain this is the Lizard in the photograph?' Daeng asked.

'Well, she does look like most other skinny old ladies,' Phosy said. 'But I'd go along with Mr Geung on this one. Siri and I are the only two who met her in person so she is aware we can identify her. The only thing in our favour is she doesn't know we've connected her to the bombing attempt. That gives us the edge.'

'I showed the photo around at the hospital today,' Dtui told them. 'None of the other patients in the picture could recall seeing her before or after that afternoon. They say she wheeled herself there and joined them at about twelve. She acted senile. Didn't get into a conversation with anyone.'

Phosy took a swig of the Thai rum generously donated by Civilai for the occasion. 'All right then,' the policeman said. 'So we know she was there at lunchtime. We also know the autopsy was delayed till five. So do we assume she was sitting there all afternoon in her wheelchair? Wouldn't some of the hospital staff have approached her to find out if she was all right?'

'Good point,' Dtui said. 'I'll ask around tomorrow. I imagine she would have been safe there until they called the other patients back into the ward. After that she would have been a bit conspicuous.'

She looked at her new husband. She was very fond of him when he was in his managerial mode. She could almost see the dials clicking over in his brain. She brushed her hand against his arm and he pulled away self-consciously.

'I'll see whether Security can give me extra copies of the wanted poster,' he said. 'It wouldn't hurt to have them placed around the hospital. It might jog someone's memory. We can write something like "If you see this woman—"'

'Shoot her!' Dtui cut in.

'I was thinking more of "Please report her to hospital officials" or something, just in case she tries again. It might help if we knew where she got the dead body from. We can't do anything about that until somebody reports him missing.'

'And the problem with that,' Civilai said, 'is that nobody trusts the police enough to report a missing relative.'

Phosy nodded. 'I imagine the Lizard selected someone who wouldn't be missed in a hurry. It's odds-on she killed him. Meanwhile, we should watch our backs. I have my men guarding all of us but we still need to keep on our toes. We were all involved in messing up the Lizard's coup plans. I'll find out what background Security has on her.'

'There is one thing we do know about her that may be in our favour,' Madame Daeng suggested.

'What's that?' Civilai asked.

'She's a prima donna, a grandstander. If you think about it, she could just as easily have lobbed that hand grenade in through the window.'

'But that would have been too easy,' Dtui agreed. 'She wants us to know how clever she is.'

'Perhaps she even wants us to match wits with her,' Daeng continued. 'I'd wager she's delighted we – that is, you, Dtui – foiled this first attempt.' There was a round of applause for Dtui, who pressed her hands together into a polite *nop* and bowed her head.

'But that means her next attempt could be even harder to detect,' Phosy added.

'Well, she's met her match with this team,' said Dtui.

'Let's hope so.'

When the bottle was finished and the meeting broke up, Madame Daeng insisted on walking Civilai out to his car. As a retired elder statesman he'd been provided a vehicle for personal use and a petrol allowance. In the United States, that gift would have taken the form of a new Cadillac. In 1977 Laos it amounted to a cream Citroën with one hubcap missing.

'Are you all right to drive?' Daeng asked as he prised open the door and climbed behind the wheel.

'Why does everybody ask me that?'

'Ooh, I don't know. Perhaps the amount of drinking you've been doing lately makes them nervous.' She handed him the car keys he'd left on the table. 'You're not showing the bottle any respect. Or yourself. Are you sure you're all right?'

'I've told you . . .'

'I mean about this investigation. Given your' – she looked back to be sure none of the others had followed them to the car – 'involvement in the last coup. The Lizard . . .'

'Madame Daeng,' he said in a whisper, 'I had no personal involvement with the perpetrators of the coup. I was involved in name alone. That woman is intent on hurting good friends of mine. Please don't think I have any qualms about her being caught. This is personal. It has nothing to do with politics.'

'I'm glad to hear that.'

'And I wonder if I could ask you not to mention past indiscretions again.'

'Well, that depends, comrade.'

'On what?'

'On whether one day you might like to pay me a visit and talk about it all; how you're feeling about things. I think it's all this "not mentioning" that's driving you into your passionate affair with alcohol.'

Civilai turned the key in the ignition and pulled the starter. The car came to life with all the aggression of a food mixer. He slammed his door and smiled at her through the half-open window before heading off.

She watched him go: a man who had sacrificed his political career with one mad rush of blood to the head. Given his history, she would never really know why he'd allied himself with the coup leaders. But he'd momentarily walked the line between retirement and execution. A man that close to dying a traitor had to have ghosts. She hoped he'd come back to see her someday.

She turned and waved to the armed guards opposite her shop. Phosy had posted a watch on her, on all of them. There was another man at the back of the shop and one more would accompany Dtui back to the police compound. Daeng doubted it would do any good in the face of a serious attack but she admitted there was a good feel to having someone watch her back.

'I'll bring you boys some hot soup,' she said and walked slowly back to the shop.

6

A MUGGING IN THE OTHERWORLD

It was an alleyway dimly lit by slightly bent street lamps that had barely enough strength to turn the black night grey. The paving stones beneath his feet were ill matching, some rising abruptly from the sidewalk. Dr Siri wore sandals but his footsteps clopped like horseshoes on the stones. Chalked roughly all around were the outlines of murder-scene bodies, deformed and chilling. He was walking fast, stumbling, wheezing from the pressure on his old lungs. The walls on either side of him reached so high he could see no summit. He looked back, stumbled again. He could sense his own fear like something living and moving between the layers of his skin. He passed a dark doorway, four legs and the end of a baseball bat all that was visible, the upper torsos drowned in a shadow as black as misery.

'Well, what do we have here, Danny?' a deep voice groaned from the darkness, Lao but with a New York accent. Siri hurried past and the two figures stepped out of the shadow and fell into step behind him.

A second voice: 'Looks like a Red gook to me.'

'Me too. What do you think you're doing here, Red gook?'

Siri didn't dare answer or look back. He quickened his pace but his pursuers stayed with him.

'Shit, man, are *you* lost.'

'He's looking for a girl, ain't you, commie gook? That's whatcha doing in our neighbourhood.'

'Is that right, commie?' Siri heard the slap of a baseball bat into a palm. A spitting noise. But up ahead he could see the gaudy neon of a nightclub. There were people milling around in front of it only eighty yards away. If only . . . He reached for the amulet beneath his shirt.

'Hell! That ain't gonna do you no good, old man.'

'You're gonna need something bigger'n that to get past us, gook.'

'You know, Danny boy? I'd say this little guy's making his way to the Pheasant.'

The name above the nightclub door was visible now through the glare: the Silver Pheasant. It flashed thousands of coloured lightbulbs. Siri heard music. Some kind of jazz. He believed it was possible now. All he needed to do was cross the— but they were on him. They grabbed his arms and yanked him onto his back. They stood over him, one with a baseball bat held above his head. Siri could see them now, angry, menacing. They wore blue jeans and boots and were twice his size. Still alive, they would have been even bigger. But all that remained of them now was grey skeletons with enormous eyeless skulls, their clenched fists like knots of ginseng.

'They play baseball back in Commie Land, gook?'

And the bat came crashing down.

Siri gasped and his head wrenched to one side to avoid the blow. And he smelled stew and death. And suddenly there was no dark street or skeletons in blue jeans. Just a room with split bamboo walls and light streaming in through gaps in a thatched roof in need of repair. He was lying on a bamboo platform above a dirt floor where a fine white long-haired dog sat staring at him. Small black pigs grunted and scurried around aimlessly. Siri was damp with sweat but not harmed. He'd been dressed in a quilted military topcoat against the cold. He felt drowsy and a little nauseous, which he attributed to some form of sedative. All around him was that unmistakable smell he knew so well from the morgue.

He got carefully to his feet and stepped down onto the packed earth. He removed the coat and laid it behind him on his bedding. His sleeping berth was no more than a large hutch in a house with four or five similar compartments. Against the walls stood farming implements, large cane baskets, one or two crossbows, and a large foot-operated rice crusher. A small family altar to the house spirits took pride of place on a shelf opposite the front door. He walked around his hutch and into the main area of the house where the central pillar rose up to the rafters. And tied to that pillar was an old woman. She was dressed in a beautiful ornate, hand-embroidered Hmong costume: a black, long-sleeved jacket and a heavy pleated skirt that came to her knobby knees. A single silver torque at her neck almost doubled her weight.

There was no question she was dead. Despite attempts to mask the smell with burning incense and candles there was no mistaking it. Either she had already begun to shrink or the costume was too big for her. Her head receded into the collar like that of a frightened tortoise. Siri had been to Hmong houses where the deceased was laid out on a platform before the funeral but had never seen a corpse suspended from the house post. She was high enough for the pigs not to reach her feet but Siri wondered why the dog hadn't made a play for her. Hungry dogs are most insensitive to the sanctity of human death.

He left the stench behind him and walked out through the open doorway to a splendid vista across a range of rolling hills. The air was so fresh and biting it brought on a coughing fit. The sun battled with the winter chill to maintain a pleasant mean. He was in a village. There was no gate or fence. There were some fifteen wooden or bamboo huts similar to but smaller than the one he'd come from. There was a chicken coop, a large cage full of mynah birds, and what he imagined to be a stable, albeit an empty one. The village land had been cleared of trees but behind the huts a mountain continued upward to a point where it was topped with vegetation like a bad haircut. Water flowed to each house from a higher source along a network of bamboo guttering. More pigs and dogs mingled with goats and the odd cow like mismatched party guests – but there were no people.

He called out a hello that echoed across the hills but received only an *oink* in reply. This kidnapping had a very casual feel to it. As there was no guard to overpower or horse to flee on, he decided to look around. All the other houses were shut up, the doors secured with chains and large padlocks. Behind one of the huts was a small copse of tall trees, the tallest of which had been left standing untrimmed. It was lavishly decorated with coloured ribbons and sparkly tin and surrounded with little offerings. This, Siri knew, was the sanctuary for the spirits of the land and the trees that the Hmong had taken. Allowing them the tallest of the trees was a sort of compromise, much better than having them haunt your house.

Having no desire to go back to spend time with his suspended housemate, Siri followed the bamboo pipes in search of the water source. He decided an icy bath was exactly what he needed to shake away the effects of the anaesthetic. As he climbed the hill and neared the foliage, cold winds seemed to surf across the mountaintops and cut through him like the reaper's scythe. Entering the trees was like crossing some official temperature median. It became eerily cold and silent. Something seemed to be sending him a warning. The amulet around his neck buzzed against his flesh.

No more than twenty yards along the forested track there appeared one more small house off to the side. It was buried deep in vegetation with only the front visible through a tunnel of overhanging trees and dangling vines. Siri had never seen an isolated hut in a Hmong village. The inhabitants liked to group closely together for safety and social cohesion. There was no advantage in living separately. He left the well-worn track and approached the house. As he got closer, he began to feel a peculiar sensation. There was a sort of physical presence, not spiritual, not the usual friendly house and field spirits that protected the Hmong, but a tangible threat. It was as if the vegetation around him seethed with resentment. The pathway through the arched trees leading to the house was barred with a symbolic fence of interwoven bamboo latticework. It was grotesquely daubed with dried blood and chicken feathers. This too Siri had seen before in front of the houses of Hmong suffering from sickness or of women in the throes of childbirth. It merely signalled that a visitor should not enter. But none of the fences in his memory had been this elaborate. Nor had they shown evidence of such wholesale massacre of fowl. Nor had he witnessed the presence of handmade dolls. Crudely formed from straw and sticks, they sat or lay around the fence in the hundreds. Some had begun their lives as vegetables or tarot roots, others were simple twig people.

Beyond the latticed fence, four land bridges had been erected. These small bamboo structures were miniature reconstructions of actual bridges but in this case they had no water to cross. They traditionally offered a shortcut for lost souls to return to their host. One was customary. Four suggested a hell of a lot of souls had gone missing from this particular house.

'Hello?' Siri called. 'Anyone there?' Silence. 'Do you need any help? I'm a doctor.'

He tried again in Hmong. The language flowed effortlessly off his tongue. This was one of the peculiar side effects of discovering his shaman roots. Until two years earlier, the language had remained dormant inside him like a mammoth frozen in a glacier. If his unknown parents had been Hmong, the old woman who raised him had given no indication of it. The only legacy he had from them was his eyes – greener than the lushest of grasses on the hills that rolled all around – and this language he'd never learned. But it drew no response. He thought he heard a sound – a low continuous growl – although he couldn't be certain it wasn't coming from his own head. He wondered whether the place might be deserted like all the others. There was no padlock on the door but he wasn't about to break the taboo and enter a marked house without permission.

The trail continued up into the mountain. The branches of bamboo gutter had converged to become just one single aqueduct at ground level. He followed it for another hundred yards and there he found a spring and a small rock pool. It looked coolly inviting but he had better manners than to bathe in the village water supply. Instead he removed his clothes, sat to one side of the pool, and used a long-handled gourd to ladle the icy water over himself. The sensation was exactly what his body needed. Every gourdful sent a million tiny needles into his skin, Mother Nature's own acupuncture.

The deeper he plunged the ladle, the icier the water, the more alive he became. Then he scooped too low and brought up sand from the bottom of the pool. He was about to empty it out of the gourd when he noticed that he'd caught something other than grit. He reached into the ladle and pulled out a button. Someone had lost a light green button with two sewing holes at its centre. It wasn't an astounding discovery but something made him reach over to his shirt and slip it into the top pocket. And he thought no more of it. There was too much in his mind to invest a great deal of thought into a button. He had been abducted and had no idea where he was. He was certain there was a negative force nearby, but none of that seemed to matter. He was having a marvellous bath and as he washed the dust out of his snowy white hair he began to sing. It was a Hmong nursery rhyme he'd picked up somewhere along life's way. It seemed appropriate.

Mmmmm . . . be good and stay quiet, little baby,
Sleep well and deep,
For in only a few seconds
Father and Mother will return
From taking care of the cows.

He then ad-libbed a line of his own: *Where the bloody hell are you, Mother and Father?*

He shook the water from his hair and opened his eyes to see seven females of various shapes and sizes standing in a line watching him. The youngest was no older than twelve; the oldest in her forties. They were dressed in similar black costumes decorated with fine embroidery. They were all smiling with not the slightest flush of embarrassment. Siri, for want of any more fitting recourse, gave a low seated bow. After a slight pause the audience laughed and clapped their hands.

7

CASHEWS MAKE ME FART

Although it seemed hardly possible, the second attempt on the lives of the coup spoilers was even more dastardly than the first. And more deadly. Phosy had discovered very little about the Lizard. The photograph on the wanted poster was the result of her only arrest. It transpired that she had been caught quite by chance with a forged pass to an official event at the Monument to the Unknown Soldier. It was an award ceremony at which the Medal of the Brave, Level 2, was given posthumously to unsung heroes of the revolution: the People's Liberation Army equivalent of the Purple Heart. The government decided it needed more role models for the younger generation and was dragging old soldiers from their graves and making them celebrities.

The Lizard had brought a wreath with a card claiming that she was a representative of the Luang Nam Tha Ladies Farming Cooperative. She laid her flowers at the foot of the monument around which stood several senior Party members, the chief of the armed forces, and the president. The Lizard was just about to step back, and presumably retreat, when the unthinkable happened. Against all the odds, the actual representative from the Luang Nam Tha Cooperative was in attendance. She stepped forward to get a better look at the wreath, pointed to the interloper, and shouted, 'This woman is an impostor.'

Several officers of the presidential guard piled onto the Lizard and the dignitaries were hurried away. The lady guards of the PLA discovered that the old woman had a Smith & Wesson K-38 Combat Masterpiece strapped to one thigh beneath her traditional skirt. An inspection of the wreath revealed a time bomb buried in the leaves with less than five minutes left to run on the clock. At the nearest police station they fingerprinted the terrorist and took her photograph before loading her into a closed truck. On her way to the Security Division and inevitable torture, she had smiled at her four armed guards. Between her teeth they saw a small white capsule.

'Ricin,' she told them. 'Virtually instantaneous.'

She bit down on the capsule and swallowed it. Although the guards did their utmost to remove the capsule and revive her, she was unconscious within a minute. There was no pulse. They explained what had happened to the officials at Security and the resident medic could not find any vital signs of life.

Somewhere between the moment they laid out her body in an open cell and three the following morning the corpse disappeared. The details were a little foggy. As usual in the socialist state nobody wanted to take the blame. It wasn't until the same woman was identified from her photograph at a subsequent act of terrorism that the PLA Security Division admitted she must have been alive when they had bagged her body that night. They had no idea how that could have been. There was conjecture that the pill she consumed may have served to slow down her pulse to a point that it was almost undetectable or that she may have actually died and come back to life again. Either way several officers were demoted.

The fingerprint check produced nothing, as almost all of the fingerprint records had been destroyed by the retreating Royalists. The That Luang police station hadn't actually known what to do with them as they had no relationship with other police forces outside the country. The Vietnamese embassy staff sent a copy to Hanoi but nothing came of it.

All this had taken place long before Phosy returned from the north-east and became attached to police headquarters. Although his office was supposed to be provided copies of army security files, in reality it took a walk down Route That Luang and a cup of hot tea with the clerk at the station before he could get his hands on them. The story hadn't made it into the newspaper of course. It was negative news and the authorities held the view that the population didn't need any more of an excuse to be dissatisfied with their government. As the people knew they wouldn't be reading about murder and intrigue, very few of them bothered to read the paper at all. Although it was considered confidential and for official eyes only, Phosy had passed the report on to his wife. He believed it was helpful for her to understand just how devious their foe could be.

Now Nurse Dtui was attempting in turn to pass on the salient points of their predicament to Mr Geung. They were squashed between the shelving units in the storeroom out of earshot of the office. The auditors had been particularly animated all day as they'd reached the bottom drawer of the cabinet, which was empty but for three final sets of records, Dtui's old Thai *Movie Fan* magazines, and a concrete imprint of a bear's paw. They could smell that the end of their work at the morgue was in sight. They sounded positively jolly as they discussed their next mission. Nevertheless, Dtui kept her voice down as she drilled Geung in safety precautions.

'All I'm saying, honey,' she summarized, 'is that you have to be careful.'

'Oh . . . of the Lizard.'

'Of anything and anybody that looks different or out of place. Don't talk to any strangers. Don't accept any gifts.'

'What a . . . about from the p . . . post lady?'

The auditor's conversation stopped and Dtui listened for footsteps on the concrete floor. She heard none.

'Letters should be all right,' she continued. 'But check that you know where the parcels come from. Ask the post lady, "Where does this come from?" All right?'

'All right. A . . . and if it comes from Comrade Dr Siri ih . . . it's OK.'

'Right.'

'Th . . . the Post Lady said it was.'

'Good. If she says it comes from— What do you mean, "said"?'

'The Post Lady s . . . said the p . . . parcel came from Comrade Dr Siri.'

'When?'

'This . . . morning. Sh . . . she said it was from the north. It w . . . was to me. It had m . . . m . . . my name written on it. And Comrade Nurse Dtui. But m . . . my name was first.' He smiled with pride and held up his chin.

'You didn't open it?'

Geung laughed. 'It was for m . . . me and you.'

'I get that. But did you open it?'

'Yes.'

'What was in it?'

'Cashew cakes.'

'Did you eat any?'

'Nnno! Cashews make me f . . . fart.'

'Where did you put them?'

'. . . and burp.'

'Geung, where are they?'

'On the f . . . filing cabi . . . net.'

Dtui moved so fast Geung wasn't sure she'd ever been there. He followed. She wasn't in the cutting room or the vestibule. He eventually caught up with her in the office. She was on her knees on the file-littered floor beside one of the auditors. Both men appeared to be taking a nap. There was froth around their mouths as if they'd just cleaned their teeth and not rinsed. The cashew cake box was upside down on the ground. Dtui was taking one man's pulse, raising his eyelid. From the expression on her face it was evident the men weren't really asleep at all.

'Th . . . they're dead?' he asked.

'Yes, pal. Dead as Uncle Ho.'

At that evening's meeting, Phosy summed up the events of the day for the team. The box and its brown-paper wrapping with Dr Siri's careful but barely legible handwriting were undoubtedly genuine. The parcel had been postmarked November 29, two days after Siri arrived in Xiang Khouang. According to the central Bureau de Poste, as there were so many VIPs in the north, the Xiang Khouang office had doubled its efforts to distribute mail daily. The package would therefore have travelled on the army transport the following day. As the clerk at Mahosot collected the hospital's mail each morning, the parcel more than likely arrived in the mail room – actually a spare desk in the clerk's office – on the first of December. That was the day of the bombing attempt. Somewhere amongst her other duties, the hospital mail clerk would get around to checking names against the list of patients and pencil in the ward or department number. The duty orderly known to Mr Geung as the Post Lady would then distribute the mail the following morning.

As she certainly wasn't in Xiang Khouang during that period and as she had very good reason not to go near the Bureau de Poste, the Lizard had to have intercepted the parcel in the mail room on the day she planned to blow up the coroner. As his name was marked on the package as sender, she had to know the doctor wouldn't be there. She probably took the parcel hoping she'd be able to do some more damage with it. She had carefully removed the wrapping and interfered with the contents. At the Lycée Vientiane, Teacher Oum was currently experimenting with Dr Siri's famous colour tests to determine what poison was used. She'd told them she'd get back to them in the morning.

The clerk had no recollection of the parcel either disappearing or reappearing, although she remembered pencilling in the morgue building number when it first arrived. She admitted she has spent most of her day out of the office but as the Lizard's photograph had been posted all around the hospital, it would have to be assumed the woman had used an accomplice to return Dr Siri's package to the unattended parcels pile.

Phosy, Dtui, Madame Daeng, and Civilai sat in silence around the slightly warped table. Although there was nothing more they could have done, they all, unreasonably, felt responsible for the auditors' deaths. Mr Geung was taking it worse than any of the others and hadn't spoken since the bodies were discovered. They knew they should have been more careful. They should have warned the clerk to look out for strange packages. But a parcel from Dr Siri himself? How could any of them have suspected . . . ?

'So, to sum up,' Civilai said, 'we're no better off than we were last meeting and we're two auditors short. We don't know anything new apart from the fact that the Lizard may or may not have an accomplice – more than likely an entire underground cell.'

'And we have no better idea of how we can find her,' Dtui added, just to make them even more dispirited. For a while, the only sound in the small noodle shop came from the ceiling lizards slurping up parked moths, and the ice in the bucket shifting as it melted. They all jumped and their hearts skipped a beat when a woman's loud voice burst upon their meditation.

'Excuse me!'

The metal shop-front shutters pulled together like a huge concertina but tonight they were open a foot to let in some air. A well dressed woman in a traditional Lao costume was peering in through the gap. One of the armed policemen had accompanied her to the door. They all laughed to mask their embarrassment. What kind of investigation team were they to be frightened to death by an old lady?

'Sorry, love,' Daeng shouted. 'We're closed.'

'Er, at the hospital they told me I might be able to find Nurse Dtui here,' the woman's large voice belted forth.

Although this was certainly not the Lizard, there was a pervading atmosphere of nervous tension among the group. Any stranger presented a potential threat.

'Who shall I say is looking for her?' Phosy asked.

'She doesn't know me,' the woman yelled, 'but my name's Bounlan. My cousin's just getting over hepatitis at Mahosot.'

'I'm glad to hear it.'

'Thank you. It's just . . . well, I saw the poster there in the ward.'

'Have you seen her? The woman?' Phosy stood and walked over to the door. The visitor was in her sixties and wearing too much make-up. He wondered whether she was a traditional singer on her way to work.

'No,' she said. 'Well, not recently anyway.' She lowered her voice at last. 'But I know who she is.'

8

EAT, DRINK, AND BE UNFAITHFUL

It was normal for Hmong men to take their meal around the main hearth and the women to eat together at a smaller grate. But here in the main house, Siri, the seven women he'd flashed at earlier, and one man of about Siri's own age sat together in one friendly circle cross-legged on a straw mat. The pigs had been banished to the yard but a white dog paraded around the perimeter of the circle and was rewarded with titbits. The animal wouldn't have been so lucky at any other village Siri had been to. Everyone in the house had plugs of folded mint leaves protruding from their nostrils. The body of the old lady continued to hang from the main pillar. Before the meal the girls had treated her with some sweet ointment that had temporarily hidden the stink, but it wasn't long before the rotting organs overpowered the scent and all the guests were forced to plug their noses.

Siri had more questions than a new history examination paper but it was impolite to jump straight into them before the time was right. He hoped that moment would come soon because curiosity was killing him. The old man opposite was presumably the village elder. The concept of headman and leader and supervisor and such had been imposed on the hill tribes by the colonists. Left to their own devices, each household and family group would look after itself without need of a figurehead. The host had a face as leathery as a monkey's palm, spiky white hair, and a wispy moustache. He moved with difficulty, a condition Siri assessed to be due to some form of lumbago. But there was nothing wrong with his humour, and when the women had led Siri down to the house, he'd gushed over the old doctor as if the two celestial brothers had floated down on their cloud for tea. But there had been no actual conversation.

Siri had been given a cup of some herbal concoction and the old man and the seven women had set about preparing the feast. The sun was rolling over a far hill when it was finally time to eat. They lit several more candles around the corpse and set two oil lamps as the centrepieces for their dinner. Since they'd met, they'd all referred to Siri by the name of his resident spirit, Yeh Ming.

'Yeh Ming,' the old man said. 'We are honoured to have you here at our meal. Eat as much as you are able. We have rice whisky to make you as drunk as you could ever hope to be. We have more food than you could eat in two more lifetimes. And, as you see, we have many beautiful girls who . . .'

Siri interrupted him before he could say anything embarrassing.

'Can I have your name, brother?'

'I am Long,' said the elder.

He then pointed his finger at each lady in turn around the mat. The youngest was Yer. Ber was round and jolly and reminded Siri of Dtui. Bao was by far the prettiest. Chia was perhaps the oldest and had a wicked leer that Siri endeavoured to avoid. Phia was a smaller version of Ber but just as round. Dia was rather manly and Nhia seemed to belong exclusively to Elder Long. She leaned against him as he ate and topped up his bowl long before it was empty. Yer, Ber, Bao, Chia, Phia, Dia, and Nhia: Siri hadn't a chance in hell of remembering them all.

'Where are the other villagers?' Siri asked.

'What you see is what there is,' Long told him.

'The men? The children?'

'All gone.'

All this was said good-naturedly as if there were nothing mournful in their departure. It left Siri uncertain as to their fate.

'Even my dear wife, Zhong, has gone,' Long smiled, pointing to the central pillar.

'When did she pass away?'

'Just two days ago.'

'Is it normal to hang her there like that?'

'It's not unknown,' Long told him. 'If we had more space we might have laid her on a platform. But as we all sleep here together in the one house now it seemed more practical to hang her up. She always said she wanted to be close to the central beam when she went. As you know, Yeh Ming, the floor is the earth, the rafters represent heaven, so the pillar is the journey the ancestors take from life to death. This gives her a leg-up, so to speak. We'll bury her tomorrow.'

It was Siri's view that tomorrow couldn't come a moment too soon.

'It isn't the way she would have liked it, but these are odd times,' Long continued. 'I wanted to invite friends and neighbours from other villages. She was a popular woman. There would have been a few hundred people here. But . . . well, you know how things are now. Of course, my great shaman, I won't insult you by asking you to preside at the ceremony. That wouldn't be right. But we'd be glad to have you there as guest of honour. If you don't mind.'

Siri didn't actually see that he had a choice. He was a helpless captive after all. The women kept topping up his cup and filling his plate. He wondered whether the time was right yet to find out why they'd brought him there. There were courtesies and there was probably a diplomatic way for him to inquire but he didn't know what that was, so . . .

'Why am I here?' he asked.

'Aha,' said Long. 'Don't try to fool us with your trickery.'

The time obviously wasn't right. Siri tried a different tack.

'Can I ask you about my . . . abduction?' he said.

'What do you need to know?' Long asked. He was throwing back the misty white liquor as fast as the cup could be refilled and it seemed to be embalming him fast. His movements were much stiffer now and his speech was beginning to sound like a tape recorder whose batteries had run down.

'Well, I'm assuming you've brought me here deliberately. Or, rather, you've brought Yeh Ming here for some purpose. How did you know where to find me? How did you know I was on the road?'

'The music of the *geng*. The music kept track of you.'

'That's very impressive.'

'That, and the wireless. The rebel base over the ridge got hold of your route and travel plan. They told us when you'd be passing.'

Siri was a little disappointed. He liked the image of being lured to his destination like some rat from Hamelin.

'Yeh Ming seems to be something of a celebrity around these parts then,' Siri smiled.

'Oh, everywhere, Yeh Ming. Not just here. Everywhere the Hmong live they sing of you. I know you are the only one who can rid us of the evil that's come over us.'

'I was afraid you might say something like that.' Siri shook his head. 'So it was the rebels from the base who ambushed the convoy this morning?'

'Oh, no. The rebels have more important things to do. No offence.'

'So . . . ?'

'We were the kidnappers, sir,' said young Yer. It was the first time any of the women had addressed him directly.

Siri looked around the mat at the angels of innocence who smiled serenely and glowed brightly from the whisky.

'You? You organized the whole thing? The avalanche? The gun attack? The . . .' He couldn't think of the word for tranquillizer. 'The sleeping poison?'

'My general here,' said Long, pointing at Bao, one of the least likely of the group to be a fighter. Obviously, somewhere deep down Siri still believed pretty women didn't need to be good at anything. The Women's Union would have his name on a blacklist if they ever found out. It was tough being an old man from a patriarchal society in the new Laos.

'You're a formidable soldier,' he told her.

She nodded in agreement and, having been spoken to, she countered with, 'And you were a fearless foe. The orange was very tasty.'

The women all laughed. Not polite Japanese giggles but hearty real-woman belly laughs.

'And, forgive me, Yeh Ming,' said Ber. 'You're mistaken about one thing.'

'Oh?'

'It wasn't this morning we brought you here. It was yesterday.'

'Yesterday?'

'Sorry,' said General Bao. 'We mixed the potion a bit too strong. We've only used it on wild ponies before.'

They all laughed again.

'I slept for twenty-four hours? I don't usually manage more than five hours a night. It's no wonder I'm rested.'

'And who's in your bed to give you only five hours of rest?' asked Chia, which again produced a round of laughter.

The alcohol was rough but effective and the women grew prettier with every cup. Siri assumed he too was getting younger and more handsome as the evening wore on. But at some stage in the celebrations Madame Daeng entered his head. Dtui found her way in there too and Geung and the odd assortment of characters living in his house in Vientiane.

'People at home will be worried about me,' he said. 'Is there any way you could get word to my friends that I'm safe?'

'Don't worry, Yeh Ming.' Long swayed as he spoke. 'I'll get word to Vientiane through the rebels. They've got a good network.'

Siri thanked him. 'And what about the people in the motorcade with me yesterday?'

'They were unhurt,' General Bao told him. 'We aren't real soldiers. We don't kill unless it's really necessary. We fight to survive. Only one of your party got lost.'

'Lost?'

'He ran into the jungle. Your soldiers searched for him for many hours.'

'I stayed to watch,' said Phia. 'I'm fat but I can hold my breath and disappear like a hungry ghost.'

'It's true, she can,' laughed Yer.

'The soldiers gave up. They had to clear the road before it got dark. They went back the way they came.'

'The one that fled,' Siri asked. 'What did he look like?'

'He ran like a man with no backbone. His face had raspberries growing from it.'

'Judge Haeng,' said Siri to himself. 'Do you know where he went?'

'I watched for a long time, Yeh Ming. He had no sense of direction. The soldiers called and he went the opposite way. He's probably still walking in circles.'

'But any man with instincts can survive up here,' General Bao pointed out.

It struck Siri that the type of instincts employed by the judge probably wouldn't help him. And he'd been alone in the forest for two days. Although Siri had admired the heroes of French literature during his studies, he'd secretly envied the callousness of the villains. Fantômas and Thénardier were so completely without scruples they must have enjoyed remorse-free lives. Siri often regretted having morals. This was one of those occasions. He briefly imagined the young judge being eaten alive by red ants or stung by the lethal toothbrush spider. Would life be better at the morgue without him? Probably not. They'd bring in another prodigy from the Eastern Bloc and Siri would have to start the training all over again. He had no choice.

'The boy in the jungle with the raspberry face is Yeh Ming's assistant,' he said. 'Without him I cannot perform . . . whatever it is I've been brought here to perform.'

'Are you sure, Yeh Ming?' General Bao asked. 'He couldn't even help himself.'

'That's true,' said Siri. 'But a great shaman has to have a

weak-minded person in his entourage to . . . to confuse the spirits. Empty vessels make the most sound, don't forget.'

'All right,' said Bao. 'If you say so, Yeh Ming. We'll look for him tomorrow, after the funeral.'

'Don't take too many of my troops,' slurred Elder Long, who was teetering on the edge of consciousness. 'We have to finish tapping the opium before we leave.'

'You're leaving?'

'Ah, Yeh Ming, Yeh Ming. Why do you play with us like this? You see all and you know all.'

'No, actually I . . .'

'I see. You want us to understand ourselves by speaking out.'

'No, I really . . .'

'No problem, Yeh Ming. I respect your wisdom. Soon the end is coming for all of us. We chose the wrong side. Or the wrong side chose us. Whatever! We have to leave. So many of our brothers and sisters have joined the big march to escape the land of the Red Dragon. Soon it'll be our turn. Turfed out again by the bastards.'

His girlfriend, Nhia, whispered something in his ear and he pushed her gently away.

'I am not. I am not drunk,' he said, waving his arm around in front of him like the trunk of a mad elephant. 'And if I am drunk it's only because I'm in the presence of the great Yeh Ming, and because my sweet wife' – he raised his cup to her and dropped it on his lap – 'is dead and smelling like a rotten foot too long in a boot. And because I have to walk a million mountains to another place that doesn't want me.'

'Where are you going?' Siri asked, hoping to get a few more snippets of information before the old man collapsed, but it was too late. Long buried his head in Nhia's bosom and sobbed.

'To America,' Bao told him.

'You're walking to America?'

'Only as far as the anarchists across the Mekhong,' Chia said. 'They say it's easy from there. "Look hungry and helpless, say you worship the big American chief, say you hate communists." And there you are in a rocket flying to the other side of the earth. Never have to work again.'

'Or live. Or be yourself,' said Long, emerging briefly from his bosom.

Nhia pulled his head back to her soft chest and continued to whisper in his ear. It was a sad moment. Siri looked down at his plate. It was piled high as the sacred mountain at Phu Bia with pork and chicken. His glass was filled to overflowing. A woman on each side of him had hold of a thigh as if they were about to make a wish and split him in two. And suddenly he was afraid.

For whatever reason, these people, these fine friendly people, had gone to a great deal of trouble to bring him here and he was afraid he wouldn't be able to help them. He wasn't a shaman. He didn't know the rituals or the rites. He couldn't bring them peace or happiness before they set off on their big walk. After seventy-three years he'd barely brought peace and happiness to himself. He knew he was going to disappoint them and, all of a sudden, he felt like a charlatan. Guilt sobered him. He politely removed the hands from his thighs, nodded at the still-full banquet mat, and got unsteadily to his feet. Long seemed to be asleep on the pillow of his girlfriend's chest.

Siri walked to the doorway, removed his nose plugs, and breathed in the fresh cold mountain air. The moon hung over the village puffing out its cheeks and varnishing the hilltops all the way to Vietnam with a warm yellow glow. Nobody should ever have to leave such a beautiful place.

'The latrine's over there.'

Siri turned to see General Bao pointing towards a dark fence. It stood out as if some celestial dressmaker had cut a rectangle from the hem of the star-filled sky. Emptying his bladder hadn't been the reason for his exit but contact with the chill air suddenly made it feel like a good idea. He negotiated a seemingly bottomless pit designed for people with unnaturally wide stances, did his business, and returned to find Bao still standing there.

'Would you like to see the shaman's house?' she asked.

'You had a shaman here? What happened to him?'

They walked together across the moonlit village compound.

'They called it "fire from a friend". This village was in a Vang Pao area. It was clearly marked on the maps. We were American. But sometimes the Lao who flew the American planes were afraid to get too close to the PL anti-aircraft guns. If it was a Hmong pilot there was no problem. The Hmong are fearless. But the Lao Royalists, sometimes they got confused. They dropped their bombs any old where so they didn't have to go back to the air base at Long Chen still carrying them. There's a lot of empty land out here. Dropping a bomb usually doesn't hurt anyone but the plants and the animals. And the plants and the animals are used to getting hurt. Our shaman, Neng, had never wanted to be a shaman. You know how it works.'

They arrived at the furthest house and Bao produced a ring of keys from her belt. She tried them one by one in the lock.

'You don't opt to be a shaman,' she went on. 'You get sick one time with an illness you can't fix with medicine. And you have a choice. You die or you become a shaman. A learned man came from another village and gave him the ultimatum. Neng wasn't in a hurry to die so he went for the second choice. Who wouldn't? He'd been a good silver worker before, but suddenly he had to spend all his time with the ills and craziness of the village. We all loved him, actually. He was good at it. Neng wasn't just playing the part. He took it seriously. He used his common sense to fix small problems, not wanting to bother the spirits for minor matters. But when it came to sickness and deep troubles of the heart and soul, he was really in control. He studied hard with his shaman master so he could be the best at what he did.'

The lock found a key that pleased it and the padlock sprang open.

'Then one day he went down to the valley to collect herbs and he was blown to bits by our side. I mean, you have to really upset some god for that to happen, don't you think? All that land. All those hills. One little man, but "boom".'

The chain dropped onto the earth where Bao's tears had already dampened the dust.

'You were close to him,' Siri said.

'He was my father.'

Siri put his arm around her shoulder and let some of her sadness soak into him. The door to the house swung inward.

'We should have brought a lamp with us,' Siri said.

'No worries, Yeh Ming.' She reached inside the door. 'This village has more Zippos than any other in Laos.'

Her hand returned, holding a colourful lighter that sported the image of a buxom girl in a bikini.

'America Number One,' she said in English, and walked into the house. It smelled of incense and rotten fruit. Siri followed her.

'When was the last time you were here?' he asked.

'Me? The day Father went to all the points of the compass.'

'And your mother?'

'She died giving birth to me.'

The Zippo lit a radius of four yards and Siri knew it had to be getting hot in Bao's hand. But she appeared to have a set destination so he followed the halo to the far side of the house. They arrived at an altar. Bao's father had gone to a lot of trouble to make it the most elaborate Siri had ever seen. It consisted of three wooden tiers. On the bottom shelf was a silver bowl containing water. Several unspun cotton threads looped from it up to the crossbeam of the house. There were handmade flowers attached to the frame and several horns of various sizes. A string of pig jaws hung from the overhead. There were three porcelain bowls of uneaten offerings on the second shelf and a solitary incense stick burning slowly.

'Someone's been here,' Siri said.

'Long! He comes every morning to worship . . . that.'

On the top tier of the altar in the place of honour was a child's toy. Hundreds of white strings led off from it like calcified veins. Spirit money was attached to it here and there and the wax of pig-fat candles clogged its frame. It was so totally incongruous it took Siri a while to identify it. Most Lao would never have seen such a thing but Siri had spent time overseas. The French called them *échasses à ressort* and it was probably the last thing one would expect to see in a Hmong village in the remote hills of Xiang Khouang, give or take, perhaps, a lawn mower.

'You know what it is?' she asked. She took three more incense sticks from a box and started to light them in the flame of the Zippo.

'Actually I do,' he told her. 'A pogo stick. How did it get here?'

'Shh, Yeh Ming. Not here.'

She lit a candle, placed the incense in a jam jar in front of the toy, and pressed her palms together in supplication. Siri wasn't about to join her.

9

FRIENDLY FIRE AND BRIMSTONE

'So, what was all that about?' Siri asked.

They sat on a log in front of the shaman's house.

'It's not my place to talk about it,' she told him.

'Really? Well, Long is unconscious so that only leaves you to explain all this,' Siri said. He could feel her reluctance to speak. 'And don't forget I'm an honoured guest.'

She looked at him at first with a rebellious expression that was soon melted by his magical eyes. She sniffed and gazed out at the eastern stars in the black map of the universe.

'We were just another village,' she began. 'Families, happy enough, working hard but surviving. We weren't interested in anything outside this mountain or the mountain before it or the one before that. Whatever place we chose was our world. But your world kept bumping into ours. You made us grow opium, then taxed us for it. You counted us and put our names in a book and forced your ways on us. It wasn't fair. We didn't interfere with anyone. But then the Americans came and asked us to give them our strongest men. Why? We needed them to work the fields but the Americans offered them money and that money bought silver. It was a fortune to us. And they gave the men guns and pretty uniforms, so they went. And some trained to be warriors, and when they came back they brought us beautiful things – coffee and sacks of rice and medicines we didn't have any idea how to use. And they brought candies for the kids and coloured posters of big movie stars. It was like heaven had sprung a leak and all the good things rained down on us.'

Siri held Bao's hand as she shook.

'Then it started,' she said. 'Chia's elder brother came home with that toy. He said he got it from his American buddy. The kids loved it. They fought over it. Brothers and sisters who'd never argued in their lives fell out over it. Even I queued up to have my turn on it. It was like a drug. My father refused to let me and I went into a sulk he never forgave me for. The stick became the centre of gravity in our world. By then, the curse was already on us. News came that two of our men had died fighting for the great American cause. Chia's brother was one of them. A recruiter came and had no trouble at all signing up six other men to join General Vang Pao, the head of the Imperial North American Force.

'They were used up in no time and the recruiter came back. He lowered the enlistment age to fifteen so our brothers went with him to get their gum and their girlie magazines and their Zippo lighters. That was when my father realized what was happening. The stick had brought a curse to our world. Since it arrived we'd lost our men and our boys and our souls. He confiscated it and the younger children hated him for it. Never before had children dared speak like that to a shaman. He knew then that evil had been reincarnated in the frame of the jumping stick. At first he buried it and used his strongest spell to remove its power over us. But still the recruiters came and this time they took our younger brothers, only twelve and thirteen. And they were all used up too.

'The stick was stronger than my father. It couldn't be destroyed. It had to be adored. For the survival of the village we had to pay homage to it. It had stolen all our menfolk and our boys. If we didn't worship it, my father was sure it would take us all. He had us line up and beg the stick to spare our lives. And it seemed to work. There were no more reports of deaths and no more recruiters came. But it needed just one more sacrifice to satisfy it. So it took my father.'

She sighed as if she'd been allowed to put down a heavy pack after a long trek.

'Is that why you brought me to your village?'

'For the stick? We all believe it's connected somehow, but, no, Yeh Ming. Not for the stick.'

'Then why?'

'Surely you know. Elder Long has forbidden us to talk about it.'

'I have no idea.'

'He said you'd know it – sense it.'

'Bao, I'm a doctor of scientific medicine. I'm not a shaman. Yeh Ming isn't my name. I'm Dr Siri Paiboun. I'm just a sort of living, breathing container for Yeh Ming's spirit. I can't even talk to him.'

A look of horror came over her face.

'But everyone has so much faith in you.'

'I'm sorry.'

For a long while the only sound was the chirruping of night insects and water dripping into the house jar. Siri broke the deadlock.

'Look. I do have some . . . connection to the spirits. I see them. I can't control them at all but I see them. Sometimes they give me clues.'

'Clues?'

'You know? Hints. I have to work out what they mean. Perhaps if you told me why I'm here I could see whether . . .'

'Yes, Yeh Ming.' She didn't seem at all heartened by this suggestion. 'Let's try that. Do you think . . . ?'

'Think what?'

'Do you think we can keep this from Long and the others? There have been so many catastrophes. This is the first time I've seen them happy for such a long time.'

'How do you suggest I do that?'

'Just pretend. Pretend you have all the powers of Yeh Ming.'

'They'll find out soon enough.'

'Perhaps. But let them have hope for now. There isn't much of that around here. Give their hearts a lift until we've buried Auntie Zhong. Then I'll tell you why we're here and see if your science and medicine can help us at all. Can we do that?'

'If you think it will help.'

'I do. Now I think we should get back. Your sleeping partner will think I've stolen you from her.'

Siri froze halfway between a sit and a stand.

'My what?'

'Ber. She'll keep you warm tonight.'

Siri sat back down.

'Actually, I don't suffer from the cold. Don't feel it at all, in fact.'

'We all sleep together, guests included. There's nothing sexual about it. You'll offend Long if you refuse.'

'Then just this once let him be offended. I tell you what. I'll sleep here in the shaman's hut. You can make up some story . . . I don't know, say I have to absorb the spells here or something.'

'It's musty here.'

'I've slept in worse.'

'Very well. I'll get you a lamp and some bedding.' A laugh she'd been trying to suppress escaped through her nose.

'What is it?' Siri asked.

'I've never known a man with so many wrinkles to be so afraid of a little female company. It's sweet.'

He watched her scurry off across the compound. So young. So frisky and bright. And all at once the face of Madame Daeng embossed itself on the inside of his dirty old mind.

Phosy's police-issue lilac Vespa seemed grateful for the fact that it only had one small hill to negotiate on its journey out to the National Pedagogical Institute at Dong Dok. With Dtui riding sidesaddle on the back it had a lot to prove. Each pop of its motor was like a small blood vessel bursting. Both riders had scarves across their mouths and noses to keep out the dust that seemed to hover above the roads for hours after the passing of each army truck.

Dong Dok was the next logical stage in the Lizard hunt. The previous evening they'd listened to their visitor, Bounlan, tell of her studies at the English Department of the nearest thing Laos had to a university. In 1964, she and thirty other teachers from around the country had been invited to the new Pedagogical Institute for a six-month course to upgrade the standard of their teaching. The woman whose photograph was on the poster had come from somewhere in the south. If Bounlan remembered correctly, her name was Phonhong, although most of the students called her by her nickname, Dtook. It was obvious she came from an affluent family as she always dressed in the most brilliant white shirts and spectacular *phasin* skirts that were probably made from antique cloth. The woman's father, Bounlan recalled, had held a senior position in government at some stage, although the family's surname escaped her. She had no idea why the woman had chosen a career in teaching. They weren't the closest of friends. In fact Dtook had kept herself very much to herself.

Phosy wondered about the woman's age. Bounlan pointed out that Dtook had always looked haggard but that she was probably no older than forty at the time they met. She wasn't an attractive woman. She always had that up-all-night-studying look. That's why the other women had been so surprised that she'd found herself such a prize husband. She'd even brought him along to the course graduation. A tall, strapping officer in the Royal Lao Army to boot.

The graduation party, Bounlan told them, was the last time she'd seen Dtook. She had no idea what had become of her. None of her classmates heard from her. Bounlan, on the contrary, was very involved in organizing reunions with the women who'd taken the course. She knew the current teachers – the *ajans* – very well. Only one who had taught the class of '64 was still on the faculty. He had been a lecturer and home teacher and he was currently the vice director of languages in the new progressive, socialist Dong Dok. His name was Ajan Ming and Bounlan was certain he would be the best bet for following up on Dtook's whereabouts. The group thanked her and noted her address in case they had any further questions.

Before Dtui and Phosy had left for the institute that morning, two peculiar items of news had come their way. The first was in the form of a note they found pinned to the morgue door. It was written in the peculiar Hmong script. Its jumbled roman characters always reminded Dtui of junior Scrabble tiles before they're arranged into real words. She couldn't make head or tail of them. They sent Geung off to find Kou, the Hmong orderly, who translated it for them.

> *Yeh Ming* – fortunately, Dtui knew who this referred to, and so, apparently, did Kou – *is alive and safe and will come back to you before the end of Hmong New Year. He is helping us. Do not worry. He is great.* It was signed *The Hmong*.

Why they had believed the note, neither Dtui nor Phosy could say. Perhaps it was the smile and knowing nods of the translator that made them feel at ease. Perhaps if the second note, this one from Manivone at the Justice Department, had arrived first, they might have been less inclined to be placated by it. If there had been no Hmong note at all they would have been frantic with worry and probably cancelled their trip to Dong Dok. The second note read:

> *Dtui,*
> *We've just learned that Dr Siri and Judge Haeng have been abducted by Hmong insurgents in Xiang Khouang. I will let you know if we get any more information. We're all praying for Dr Siri's safe return. Manivone*

If she hadn't read the Hmong note first, Dtui wouldn't have noticed the omission of Judge Haeng in the Justice

Department prayers. As it was, both she and Phosy were still chuckling about it when they left. They could think of no reason why the Hmong would bother to deliver the note unless it was true. The mission to Dong Dok was still on.

They'd tried to phone ahead several times but as the Lao said, passing a live turtle up one nostril and down the other was easier than trying to make a local telephone call beyond the city. It was only ten kilometres to Dong Dok but it might as well have been in another solar system. Civilai hadn't wanted Dtui and Phosy to venture there. He wanted them somewhere safe until the Lizard had been caught but of course they would have none of it. Their armed guards accompanied them to the edge of town, but once they were certain they weren't being followed, the pair insisted on going on alone. Stubborn as teak roots, the pair of them. So there they were putt-putting past the ramshackle roadside stalls, to the front gates of Laos's seat of higher learning.

The only building visible from the road was a French-built two-storey off-white construction with an impressive roof that had probably made the locals go 'ooh' when it was being built, but that didn't hold a candle to even the most provincial college in France. It was the administration block whose offices let onto an open-air balcony, like a seaside hotel. Goats chomped unenthusiastically at the thick grass around its base. Phosy paused to ask directions from the guard in the little concrete booth at the gate. The drowsy man apologized and said he didn't know because he was a postman just taking a nap there in the empty box. A passing student overheard their question and pointed them straight ahead.

It was such a silent place that the roar of their small motor embarrassed them. They could imagine lectures in the modest huts coming to a halt until they'd passed. More goats looked up and chickens tested their chicken skills by scurrying in front of the Vespa at the last second. They passed whole shanties of student dormitory shacks made of rattan and tin and finally came to the back gate. The building beside it had a handwritten wooden sign attached that announced ENGLISH DEPARTMENT.

They were climbing off the bike when a rather distinguished-looking man with curly hair dyed black walked past them. He had a stack of books under his arm. He ignored the visitors at first but curiosity seemed to pull him back.

'May I help you?' he asked. His voice was deep and syrupy.

'Yes, we were hoping to find Ajan Ming,' Phosy said.

'Is that so? Then you must have consumed your lucky medicine this morning.'

'Because?'

'Because I am he.'

Phosy and Dtui introduced themselves and briefly explained why they were there. Ajan Ming told them he was on his break and invited them to a slightly leaning building just beyond the back gate where coffee was sold. They sat at a table by a large rectangular hole in the bamboo wall. As they spoke, Dtui's gaze returned from time to time to an elderly lady in rags who swept and reswept the dirt path opposite. She wore a conical hat that left her face in shadow.

'Don't you think?'

Ajan Ming's question had been directed at Dtui. She turned away from the window.

'I'm sorry?'

'I said it would be unfortunate if we were held responsible for every student we teach once they leave our institution. It wouldn't make any more sense than your being taken to task for your former patients getting into trouble.'

'You're quite right,' she said. She turned back to the window but the woman was gone.

'You do your best for them, then they're on their own. And she was just a teacher in a refresher course. It's not as if we'd acquired them fresh from the lycée.'

'But it was your first course.'

'My first here at Dong Dok but I'd been teaching at the Normal School in Vang Vieng beforehand.'

'But you do remember this Phonhong?'

'I have an excellent memory. I remember all my old students, no matter how short the course. And in this case I have good cause to remember her.'

The *ajan*'s spectacles seemed to be giving him a headache so he took them off and put them in the top pocket of his shirt. Three hot gooey coffees with condensed milk foundations arrived in unholdable glasses.

'Why is that, Ajan?'

'Well, it was soon quite apparent that she was a fanatical Royalist. I imagine her family had some royal connections although she didn't boast about it. As you know, in the old days, if a family had money they'd send their children to study in France or one of the English-speaking countries. But it appeared Phonhong had done all of her studies here so the highest level she could achieve was teaching in a regional school. I asked her why that was and she told me she had devoted herself to the betterment of her people. She wanted to show the Lao that one didn't have to go abroad to get an education, which wasn't completely true. But I admired her resolve.'

'Did you have any trouble with her when she was here?' Dtui asked, churning the coffee and milk together with a weightless tin spoon.

'Not trouble exactly,' Ming told her. 'She started a club for undergraduate students. It was an anticommunist club. I can't recall precisely what they called it. She spread the word that the Red plague would one day engulf our country and destroy all the good work the Royalists had done. Much as I love our great socialist state, there are those who would describe that as something of a prophecy a decade ago.'

'Did the group do any agitating?' Phosy asked.

'Not really. They just put up posters warning of the Red threat and held rallies.'

'Can you recall who else was in that club?' Phosy asked.

'Not offhand. I could put together a list for you as it comes to me, I suppose.'

'We'd be grateful. Did you have any contact with her after she graduated?'

'Nothing personal,' Ming confessed, 'but this is a small country. I was kept in touch with her activities by others. As you know, everybody knows someone who knows someone here.'

'What did you hear?'

'They had a son, she and her soldier husband. She'd raised him as a patriot. As he was going through his teens the war against the communists was heating up. He too enlisted in the military and by fate or influence he found his way into his father's regiment. Rumour has it that they were on a mission together in Huaphan in the north-east and that both father and son were slaughtered in a PL ambush.'

Dtui's gaze flicked back from the window.

'Now that would be enough to make a woman nuts,' she said.

Ajan Ming seemed a little taken aback by her insensitivity.

'I'm sorry,' she said. 'Please go on.'

'That was the end of the story. We heard no more of her.'

'And you don't recall the family name of the soldier?' Phosy asked.

'Not at all.' The coffee was barely cool enough to sip but he held the glass in a paper napkin and threw back the entire contents in one gulp. 'That doesn't help you, does it?'

'No.'

'I wish there were some way I could make a connection for— Ah, now there's a possibility.'

'What is?' Dtui asked.

'They were Christian. The whole family. Catholic if my memory serves me right. Phonhong had converted when she married the officer. If the husband and son had a Christian funeral—'

'They'd be buried in the Catholic cemetery. Brilliant,' said Phosy.

'If only we knew their names.' Dtui shook her head.

'But we do,' said Ming, glowing with that righteous radiance intellectuals exhibit when they solve problems. 'Their first names, at least. Both the husband and son had been named after the great king Fa Ngum. That shouldn't be too hard to find on a headstone.'

'Excellent.' Dtui smiled. 'I should spend some time out here. Maybe some of this brilliance would rub off on me.' She wrote down the name and one or two notes to herself on a napkin.

'Let's go take a look,' Phosy suggested.

'What now?'

'No time like the present. It isn't the biggest cemetery in the world.'

'Not the biggest at all,' Ming agreed. 'I confess you two have me worked up into such a lather I'd even consider going with you to conduct the search. Unfortunately, I have to proctor an examination in the next hour.'

'Ajan Ming, you've done more than enough already,' Phosy told him. 'We can handle it from here. Thank you.'

Dtui looked anxious. 'Shouldn't we get in touch with the others?'

'Come on, Dtui,' Phosy laughed. 'To look around a cemetery? What trouble can we get into there?' He shook his head at Ming. 'I'm afraid my wife's getting a little paranoid in her old age.'

'Paranoia isn't always a bad thing,' Ming responded them. 'But I am assured the residents of the Catholic cemetery are harmless.'

'Then at least let's stop for lunch on the way,' Dtui pleaded. 'I'm not sure I can go rooting through a cemetery on an empty stomach.'

10

NON-PRACTISING ATHEISTS

According to official work application forms and Party records of affiliation with organizations, Phosy and Dtui were atheists. Not surprisingly, anyone who filled in a form in the People's Democratic Republic checked 'atheist' in the religion box. It was circumspect to do so: 'opium of the people' and all that. But the Lord Buddha isn't a deity who just goes away when you fill in a form. There were very few Lao who didn't offer him their thanks on the rare occasion when things went right. His was a good old-fashioned religion that didn't cause wars or advocate hatred of the beliefs of others. And, at the end of the eightfold path, a Buddhist could expect his remains to be barbecued to the size of a pillbox and placed on the family altar.

So, for two latent Buddhists like Phosy and Dtui to be strolling around a Christian graveyard in the heat of the midday sun was a little overwhelming. Only a few feet below them lay the complete and nicely dressed remains of hundreds of God worshippers, any one of whom could break through the earth and wrap his or her bony fingers around the trespassers' necks, just like in the movies.

'I'm not sure I can do this,' Dtui confessed.

'Take a deep breath.'

The Vientiane Catholic Cemetery was out on route 13 at kilometre 9. It was a walled field and most of the graves and stones were squashed to one end as if for warmth or companionship. The occupants were a peculiar mix of European, Chinese, and Lao, the planners had given the bodies very little space to stretch out and relax in the after-life. Phosy had never learned Western script so Dtui led them from stone to stone translating as she went. Fortunately, the headstone they were looking for was in the first corner of the cemetery they searched. They'd headed for the newest-looking stones and the best-kept plots. The wide plot had one headstone for both father and son. It was inscribed in English: 'Here lie two Warriors named Fa Ngum. May their Souls rest in Peace.'

'Well, that's marvellous,' said Dtui in her loud huffy voice. 'Now what are we supposed to do, interview them?'

She kept the thought to herself that this was exactly the situation in which you could use a Dr Siri, communicator with the dead. She knew her husband wasn't a great fan of superstitious mumbo jumbo. They gazed around. There appeared to be no office. One elderly gentleman with long unkempt hair stood glaring at a headstone. He held a bouquet of lifeless flowers in front of his crotch. In the next row a worker with a long-handled rake removed leaves from the walkway. He was a short man with sunburned skin and unkempt whiskers growing in thickets here and there across his chin. His smile was no more than a single drawn line on a cartoon face but it made him look like a man who enjoyed his work.

Phosy called over to him. 'I was wondering . . . ?'

'Good health,' the man said, his smile opening to show a full set of white teeth.

'Good health. I wanted to know if there might be an administration office somewhere where we could inquire about a grave here.'

'Used to be, sir. Shut down when the French left. There's just me now.'

'For the whole place?'

'Yes, sir. They don't cause me a lot of trouble.'

Phosy walked between the graves to join the worker. Dtui held back and looked discreetly at the mourner. The old man hadn't put down his flowers. He was standing there either mouthing a prayer or inflicting a curse.

'Have you been here long?' Phosy asked the worker.

'Twenty seven years, sir.'

'Really? So who pays your salary now that there are no French?'

'There's a fund. The bereaved pay into it for the upkeep. No graves to dig these days, just trimming grass and cleaning up.'

'Then you'd know a thing or two about the graves?'

'Yes, sir. More than a thing or two no doubt. What one was you interested in?'

'The two Fa Ngums.'

'Oh, yes, sir. Tragic! Just tragic. Father and son massacred on the same day.'

'Does the boy's mother, the wife of the officer, does she come to pay her respects?'

'Yes.' He nodded at Dtui, who'd joined them. 'Good health, ma'am.'

'When was the last time you saw her?' she asked.

'Ooh, let me see. Must have been a few weeks ago. Yes, that'd be right. She travels a lot, I believe. Lovely woman.'

'So she's here often?'

'Yes, ma'am. Could turn up at any time.'

Dtui felt the whisper of premonition shudder through her bones.

'Would you happen to know whether there's a record of who pays for the stones and contributes to the upkeep?' Phosy asked.

'Ooh, that would have been with the French curate, sir. Long gone, I'm afraid. No idea where that'd be now.'

'So there's no way we could contact Fa Ngum's wife?' Dtui said.

'Tell the truth, ma'am, the ledger wouldn't have helped anyway in such a case.'

'It didn't have names and addresses?'

'Oh, indeed it did, but she wasn't the one what paid. It was the older lady. The soldier's mother who took it upon herself. She's getting on a bit now.'

'You know her?'

'Yes, sir. Had to go by her place once or twice to pick up wreaths.'

'Then, you know where she lives?'

'Oh, yes. It's that big old mansion down by Wat Tai on the river. She lives there by herself now.'

'Excellent.' Phosy smiled. 'We're very much obliged to you, comrade.'

'You're welcome, sir, ma'am.'

The worker bowed politely and returned to his raking.

'What do you say?' Phosy asked Dtui. 'One more stop for the day? It's on the way home.'

'Look, I don't feel comfortable wandering around with' – she lowered her voice – 'that maniac on the loose.'

'Nothing's happened to us.'

'No! But we've had armed guards all week.'

'She'd have no idea where we are. Where's your sense of adventure?'

'Sometimes you just don't think like a policeman.'

'And sometimes you think too much like one.'

'You can be very annoying, Phosy. This is positively the last stop, but only if little Malee here and her big ma can get a glass of iced tea on the way. My throat's as dry as the crypt. No offence,' she said, looking along the ordered rows of passé Frenchmen. Apart from the worker, they were alone now in this eerie place. Above ground, anyway.

The large metal gate was ajar and so clogged with weeds and vines it had apparently been open for a very long time. Phosy drove through the gap into the broad dirt yard. When he cut the motor no sounds emanated from inside the old two-storey French mansion. It was the colour of a neglected tooth. Several rows of red clay pots stood guard around it. At some stage they'd contained pretty bougainvillea and mimosa and magnolia but now their dark skeletons poked from the cracked earth in crippled poses. The wooden shutters at the front of the house were closed. At one time blue, they'd been lashed the colour of a shipwreck by the monsoons.

It was a mansion barely in the mood for visitors. If the front door hadn't been open and the front step littered with shoes paired off like parentheses, Phosy and Dtui might have given up on the place. Instead, they walked up the two large steps and peered inside.

'Good health,' Phosy called. 'Anyone home?'

They heard the distant voice of a woman.

'We're out back,' she shouted. 'Come on through.'

In a Lao house, before the days of suspicion and paranoia,

this had been a normal thing. No chain locks or spy holes. A visitor received a friendly welcome no matter how dirty his feet or empty his belly.

'Just two new friends,' Dtui called as they walked through the large open-plan front room that smelled to Phosy like muddy football boots left to dry in the sun. There was dust in the air.

'Out here! Just follow my voice,' the woman called.

Dtui and Phosy arrived at a large well-lit kitchen. Three unshuttered windows opened onto a jungle of a backyard. An old lady was bent over a stone sink with her back to the guests. She wore a ridiculously long *phasin* and a head scarf of the type favoured by the queen of England on hunting trips.

'We're sorry to disturb you,' Dtui said.

'Oh, my dears. No problem at all,' replied the woman. As she turned she seemed to uncurl and become a lot taller than she'd first appeared. In her right hand she held an M-1911 pistol. With her left she undid the scarf and let her long gray hair fall past her shoulders. Phosy reached for Dtui's hand.

The Lizard walked confidently toward them. 'I think I'm supposed to say something like, "Aha so we meet again, Inspector Phosy." At least that's the type of thing Moriarty would have said.'

She unfastened the *phasin* and it dropped to the floor. Underneath she was wearing chic European trousers.

'But, of course, what would a Red know of literature and culture? I could say in English, "Welcome to my parlour" and even if I bothered to translate it, you still wouldn't have a clue what I'm talking about. I'm afraid this trap for common flies might appear a little over-elaborate but what terrible fun. You see, we've had little to do but twiddle our thumbs since you spoiled our nice coup d'état.'

'How could you know we'd be here?' Phosy asked, his arm around Dtui.

'Well, that's the splendour of the chase, my silly policeman. Every move you made today has been orchestrated. We challenged ourselves, you see. We wondered whether we'd be clever enough to persuade the fish to leave the sanctity of their pool and come in search of the hook. But there I go mixing my metaphors horribly – flies and fish – shame on me. Never mind.'

'Who's "we"?' Dtui asked.

'Cue the curtain call.' The woman beamed. 'The gentleman behind you— No, you may look, it isn't a trick—'

The couple turned their heads to see Ajan Ming with a Beretta framed in the doorway like an old master. He nodded politely.

'—we shall call person D.'

The door to the maid's room off the kitchen opened and through it walked Mrs Bounlan and the worker from the cemetery. They bowed and seemed disappointed not to receive a round of applause.

'Our final two cast members,' the Lizard said. 'And I think we'll use their stage names, Mr C and Miss B. And of course there's me, A – scriptwriter and extra. You know, it is terribly hard to remain humble when you're as good as we are.'

She strutted around her grounded fish, close enough for them to see the madness in her beady eyes.

'You'll notice how we were able to lure you just a little bit farther and farther from your allies, checking at each stage that you'd fallen for it hook, line, and sinker. Making certain that you hadn't contacted anyone to pass on the information you'd learned.'

B and C came to sit at the kitchen table while D held his position at the rear.

'You were interesting adversaries for a little while – very well done with the bomb thing, by the way – but enough's enough. All that's left is to decide how unpleasantly you're going to meet your respective ends. Of course, it will have to be something so terrible your super Dr Siri turns somersaults when he sees your remains. An angry foe doesn't think straight and we need him at his most vulnerable. We have something very special planned for him. It's rather a pity that you won't be around to see it.'

She turned her back on them and reached into a drawer. When she turned around she was holding a rusty fish gutter in her gnarled hand.

'Now, who's first?'

Dr Siri had become very fond of his captors as they sang and joked and prepared for the burial of Mrs Zhong. Given the amount of preparation involved and the serious absence of men who normally bore the brunt of the heavy work, it was reluctantly decided that the search for weak-minded Assistant Haeng would have to wait till late afternoon, perhaps even the following day. Siri was concerned for the life of his boss but there was nothing he could do. He knew his own lab assistant, Mr Geung, had survived several nights alone in the jungle, but Mr Geung was only mentally handicapped. He wasn't a high-court judge, a man trained to interpret and assess and deliberate. Haeng had nothing practical in his arsenal. Every dictum in the world lined up one after the next wouldn't stop a man from being eaten by a tiger. Geung would climb a tree.

Even down to the last gulp, Haeng would be citing how unconstitutional it was to consume a government official. Heavens, the man had even managed to run away from his own soldiers. If he'd survived these last few days, Siri would be astonished. But death? That's life.

And death was the business of the morning. Much of that business was dedicated to shaking off the evil spirits that, given free access, would have made off with Auntie Zhong's soul as soon as look at it. With the dark forces milling around the front door of the house like annoying press photographers, the girls surreptitiously cut a hole in the side wall and sneaked her out on a stretcher. The four bearers were dressed as men in hopes the gods wouldn't notice the digression from tradition. They bore down the hill at a cracking pace, Siri hot on their heels, hard-pressed to keep up.

The transvestite stretcher bearers would jog off in one direction, giving the impression they were heading directly for the grave. Then, Nhia, the head pall-bearer, would shout, 'Left' or 'Right' in a basso voice and the team would suddenly change direction. In rugby, this tactic was known as 'throwing a dummy'. Any pursuing spirit not fooled back at the house would be going so fast that the change of tack would hopefully send it careening on down the hillside like a puppy on waxed parquet. Just to make sure, the tactic was repeated six or seven times before they finally headed west – the ultimate direction of every burial.

By the time he'd worked out this ruse, Siri was so out of breath he sat on the hillside and watched the entourage zigzag down the hill. With a little common sense he was able to work out their final destination and arrived there at roughly the same time as Auntie Zhong. Dia was there playing the departing dirge on a *geng*. She performed with such skill her manly face assumed an air of divine beauty. The other women stood around in their finest costumes, each wearing a tiara of silver coins. A buffalo was tethered to a post near the grave and Elder Long crouched, rattling the divining horns in a large Christmas Special Hershey Bar jar. As soon as the body arrived and was lowered onto a temporary platform, he emptied the horns onto the ground. Their positioning would tell the assembled guests whether Auntie Zhong accepted the buffalo as a parting gift. As it was too dangerous to travel between villages at this time, the assembled guests amounted to the women, Siri, and a few goats.

Eight times Long cast the horns and eight times his wife rejected the buffalo. He walked over to the body, which was dressed in its very best costume – a pleated skirt that had taken six months to weave, dye, and embroider, a skirt that would be worn only once.

'You old bat,' he said playfully. 'Cantankerous to the last. It's all we have. You know I'd love to sacrifice you a whole herd of cattle but we're at the end of the livestock. Perhaps you'd like us to bring your father over and offer him to the gods?'

Siri turned to Bao. 'Her father?'

'The white dog,' she said. 'It arrived in the village one day. Hmong women are naturally suspicious of strange dogs but Zhong was certain the animal was her dead father returned from heaven. He'd been cruel to dogs all his life so she believed the gods had punished him like this. From that day till her death she spoiled the animal rotten.'

On the ninth cast of the horns, the old lady relented and the buffalo was condemned to death. Chia walked over to Siri carrying an enormous axe and handed it to him. His heart stopped. Siri, for all his faults, could not kill. Since he'd become so well acquainted with the afterlife, he'd found it impossible – mosquitoes and small underfoot insects not included – to take a life. He couldn't even bring himself to strangle a chicken or allow a fish to drown in air. But he was the only male guest and the heavens and the middle earth were counting on him to make Zhong's transition complete. He looked at the proud old beast. He really didn't want to be haunted for all eternity by a vengeful buffalo.

With the axe behind his back, he walked to the tethered animal, who chomped happily on the fresh grass around her hooves. She was probably thinking what a pleasant day out this was – music, a show, and a meal. She couldn't wait to tell the pigs when she got back.

Siri knew he had no choice. He prayed to the ancestors for a way out but nothing was immediately forthcoming. So he lofted his axe and stood before the buffalo, who suddenly realized all eyes were on her. With a beard of grass hanging from her mouth she looked up at the old man in front of her. In his hand she saw the hoisted axe and, through whatever process an ox makes connections to past events, something seemed to register in her slow brain. And when she realized what was about to happen, her heart, already heavy with hay, gave out. She keeled to one side, took one more chew of her grass, and passed away. To Elder Long it was confirmation. One more miracle. Yeh Ming had felled a buffalo with his mind. He became even more convinced that the trouble that haunted their village could be cured.

The interment that followed went according to plan. Yer, playing a pipe, and Phia, carrying a burning brand, led the bearers to the grave site. When the pipe ceased its lament, all the women screamed, laughed, and ran as fast as they could back to the hut, leaving Long and Siri alone with the body.

'What happened?' Siri asked.

'Women aren't allowed to see what happens next,' Long told him. 'How's your back?'

The two old men lifted Zhong's stretcher and carried her to an open coffin embedded in the ground. They laid her inside, broke up the bier, and put it on top of the body. While Siri burned incense and set light to the spirit papers, Long fired an arrow from a consecrated crossbow across his dead wife. He said the final prayers, they put the lid on the coffin, and covered it with earth. Siri was feeling appropriately solemn until Long smiled and slapped him on the back.

'One down, three more to go,' he said. 'Let's hope the others outlast me.'

'The other what?'

'I'm married to three more of those girls, Yeh Ming. I only wish I had the energy and the years to enjoy them all.'

Siri laughed. 'I assume Auntie Zhong knew about that.'

'It was her idea. She would have had me marry all of them but the rest share our surname. They'd lost their men. I was the only bull left in the herd. Zhong was only too pleased at the thought of having me out of her nest for a few nights a week. But I wouldn't go. Refused point-blank. Not while she was alive. We'd been together fifty years. Fifty years, Yeh Ming. You can't suddenly be unfaithful after all that time, can you now?'

Siri dwelled for a moment on his lifetime marriage to Boua. He'd felt the same way.

'You can't,' he said.

'I'll miss her.'

'She'll be glad to hear that.'

'But, now she's gone . . .'

11

BETROTHED TO A DEVIL

There had been a swine genocide that morning. Every pig in the village had been sacrificed to the spirit of Auntie Zhong. That meant pork for lunch, and buffalo which was chewy but it was packed with a lot of vitamins and life-enhancing minerals. The funeral lunch was subdued, but more from the exhaustion of the preparations than out of sadness. There was nothing to be sombre about. Assuming the gods hadn't noticed the female pall-bearers, all the steps had been laid for Zhong's journey to the afterlife. She'd had a good send-off and everyone was happy, not to mention a little envious that she was on her way to a better place.

After the meal, Dia and Chia dressed in their prettiest clothes and set off in search of weak-minded Assistant Haeng. General Bao explained that there were many PL troops out looking for the abductees and if the women were to run into a patrol dressed in army fatigues and carrying weapons, they'd be shot on sight. But in their costumes, searching for roots and twigs, they had a slightly better chance. The two scouts knew the hills far better than the soldiers so they weren't expecting to be caught by surprise. Siri and Bao watched them climb onto two sprightly ponies and waved them off.

'And you won't be going with them?' Siri asked.

The little general hadn't changed out of her man's clothes from the funeral but the sight of her still filled his heart.

'No, Yeh Ming. I have a lot to tell you. Come.'

They began to walk towards the trail that led up the mountain. 'We thought the jumping stick was on our side at last but it didn't protect us from this new evil. There were fifteen families here in the village. Three different clans but we were one unit. All friends. All caring for each other like one family. We lost our men and then we lost our war. There wasn't much hope for us to stay here. Women and children and old people aren't going to survive in an exposed place like this. The Hmong scouts told us your army will soon be getting new helicopters and bombers from the Soviets. Once that happens, even the most secluded village will be overrun. Most of our friends have left already.'

'On the big march?'

'Yes, but the strongest of us stayed behind to help Long and Zhong. They refused to leave without their daughter.'

'She's one of you seven?'

'No. You haven't seen her. She doesn't show herself to many.'

'The house beside the trail?'

Bao nodded. 'My father used to tell me of some evil presence beyond the peak of this mountain. It allowed us access to the water but we were advised to keep away from the hut and the jungle behind it. That's why we were upset when Chamee moved up here. She stays there alone. Her story is more tragic than any other. She was fourteen, quite beautiful and untouched by any man. Long and his wife had ensured that much. They wanted her to have a special marriage, but, above all, they wanted her to wait till the war was over so she didn't end up marrying a corpse. But we think it was because she was unspoiled that she was such a target. A beautiful virgin. What spirit could resist that?'

'She was possessed?'

'Much worse than that, Yeh Ming. She's betrothed.'

'To?'

'I cannot say.'

They were nearing the lonely house and all of Siri's instincts began to twang just as they had on his first trip up to the spring. He stopped and took Bao's hand.

'You know?' he said. 'That old "we can't speak its name" routine doesn't work at all. That was all made up by story-tellers to scare little children. Let's assume that I can take the pressure – spiritually. If it's a curse I know I can pretty much handle it. You have to tell me everything.'

She looked into his eyes and knew he was sincere. She lowered her voice and a tremble ran through her words.

'It is Moo'er. He is the illegitimate nephew of Xor, the thunder demon. He keeps a harem on earth and seeds them all.'

'Long's daughter's expecting a demon?'

He obviously sounded cynical because Bao cut him in half with her evil eye.

'Shame on you, Yeh Ming, for doubting such a thing.'

'It's not that I doubt, sweet general. It's only that I've never heard of a devil having the . . . equipment to achieve such a feat.'

'Then see with your own eyes.'

She paced off ahead leaving Siri no choice but to scurry after. There was no doubt in his mind that some discontent haunted the area around the old house yet he would have expected demonic impregnation to register more violently on his senses. The closer they came to the house, the warmer his amulet felt against the skin of his chest, but even as they stood no more than five yards from the lattice fence everything seemed calm.

Bao called out, 'Chamee, a great shaman has come to see you.'

There was no response.

'How do you know it's actually Moo'er and not just some other randy demon?' Siri asked.

'He told us who he was when he first came.'

'How?'

'You'll see.' She shouted again. 'Yeh Ming has come all the way from the past to exorcise your demon, Chamee.'

They stood waiting for some reaction but heard only the civets laughing in the trees overhead and the distant sound of explosions. Siri was beginning to wonder whether even Chamee was a figment of Bao's imagination when the door to the house opened slowly and a vision appeared. A young girl, even more beautiful than Bao, walked from the shadow of the house and stood in the sunlight that filtered through the leaves above. Her hair was in wild Rastafarian knots, and insomnia had charcoaled black rings around her eyes. The effect was exotic and mysteriously frightening. She wore a sheer white slip, no more than a woven cobweb, and her enormous stomach heaved against the cloth. Siri was astounded at the size of it. There were no hidden cushions to magnify the condition. The shift clung to her like lint and left no secrets. She carried the largest child he'd ever seen in his life.

'This is what frightens Long,' Bao whispered. 'If the demon child is born, his daughter will be split in two. And then Moo'er will claim his offspring and the spirit of his bride and drag them down to his world. This is why Long went to so much trouble to bring you. She hasn't eaten for a month. We bring her food but she ignores it.'

Siri had seen a good many inexplicable phenomena of late, but in spite of his spiritual afflictions, he was still a logical, scientific man – not to mention a cynic. He'd had dealings with the *Phibob*, the malevolent spirits of the forest who hounded him. And he'd realized, all too late, that the only real damage they could inflict was on his mind. That didn't make them any less dangerous but it did give him an advantage. Evil, he had come to believe, was controllable as long as man had the strength of will to believe in himself. He had never actually run across demons before but he was prepared to put his theory to the test.

He walked to the fence and, by working it back and forth, began to loosen the central post that held it up.

'Yeh Ming, I really don't think that's a good idea,' Bao said.

'Don't worry, my general. So far, it's no more than a fence.'

Chamee stood still in front of her door, a small fixed smile on her face. She seemed to be urging him on. Her hands caressed her huge belly like a fortune teller with a glass globe. The fence, being symbolic, wasn't hard to pull down. It fell in front of Siri and he stepped over it. He heard a low growl from inside the house, neither human nor animal.

'I'm just a doctor,' he said. 'Nothing to worry about. I want to take a wee look at that baby of yours.'

He stepped into the tunnel of vines and roots that hung down from the old trees on either side of the path and as he did so he felt a kind of force. The area seemed to be alive.

A strange tingle ran through his skeleton like ant bites, not painful but uncomfortable. He continued forward, swimming his arms through the vines, but he was disorientated. He stood still for a moment to clear his head but the pins and needles made his legs numb and turned into a dull ache.

He looked up at the round-bellied virgin in time to hear her speak. She was still eight yards away but her voice was loud.

'Keep coming, old man.'

He watched her lovely lips move but the sounds they uttered were deep – not possibly the voice of a teenaged Hmong girl.

'Keep coming,' she said again. The voice shocked Siri and put him on the defensive.

'You obviously don't realize who I am,' he said with more bravado than real confidence. 'I am Yeh Ming, the shaman.'

His body was shaking like a tin roof in a monsoon. His toes curled. He clenched his fists and took another step. He tried to calm her with his words.

'Come on, dear. I'll just take a look at you and then I'll leave you alone. You need a doctor. Look at the size of you.'

'Then come on,' she said, curling her finger towards him. 'I'm waiting.' Her voice was even deeper now, a frightening double-bass-string twang.

He took another step but the vines seemed to strangle him, whip at his shoulders and chest. He refused to believe that he could be physically assaulted by the spirit world in broad daylight, awake, and sober. It was impossible, but . . . He took one more half step before the air around him became a blinding flash and he was zapped like a mosquito on a truck battery. All he recalled as he floated to the earth was the sight of the pregnant girl waving at him in slow motion and the black sky wrapping him up like a newborn in a tar blanket.

'You are a hero, Yeh Ming. A hero.'

Siri's eyelids opened slowly like the remote-controlled garage doors he'd seen in the movies. The muscles in his upper torso ached. He felt like he'd been tied in a burlap sack and thrown down a flight of stairs. He wore no shirt and his chest was covered in lash wounds and bruises. Elder Long was leaning over him, smiling.

'None the worse for wear at all,' he said. He grinned and turned to the five women who sat behind him in an arc. 'Just marched on in there. Took down the fence and, brave as you like, marched on in. That's courage.'

All but General Bao were smiling.

'That's courage,' Long repeated. 'I'll warrant something knows it's got a fight on its hands now. Look out, you who cannot be named, Yeh Ming's in the village. That's the end of you.' He laughed and punched his fist into the air.

Siri rolled to his side and threw up. It was evidently not the first time. Yes, he thought, somebody did have a fight on his hands, but it was Siri himself. This was far beyond the limited realm of his experience. It wasn't a battle of wits and wills. It was a physical fight. He had no idea how to wage war against a demon, a supernatural creature who was capable of raping virgins and swatting old doctors like midges.

'We'll have the exorcism tomorrow afternoon,' Long said.

'What?' Siri groaned. 'Couldn't we put it off for a day or two?'

'Testing me again, Yeh Ming?' smiled Long.

Bao explained for Siri's benefit, 'We're coming into the week of Hmong New Year. The auxiliary spirits take a holiday. They won't be around to accompany you to the Otherworld. Tomorrow's our last chance.'

'I'm not sure I'll be well enough,' Siri said.

'Don't worry.' Now Bao smiled. 'The feeling will go away in a couple of hours. The scars last for a week.'

Siri raised his eyebrows and she nodded. She was quite a girl.

12

THE SHAMAN'S MAIDEN FLIGHT

Night had already enveloped the village and the evening meal sat undigested in Dr Siri's gut. There was only so much pork a man could eat. Still aching from his run-in with Moo'er, he sat in the shaman's hut with General Bao undergoing a crash course in how to conduct an exorcism. He'd attended them before but seeing was by no means the same as doing. He'd once seen a man twirl plates on the end of cane rods but he'd broken four when he tried it himself. Pretending to be a shaman wasn't going to be any easier. And pretend was all it could be. Siri and Bao had decided it was the least he could do for his host. Just provide a little hope, go through the motions, say, "'Sorry, Long, I did my best' and go home.

But that wasn't Dr Siri Paiboun. Deceit and trickery didn't sit well on his conscience. He had to do more than that. Earlier, while he'd sat on a boulder waiting for his supper, the sun slowly easing its way over the mountains, he'd engaged himself in a little lateral thinking like his literary hero Inspector Maigret. There was no doubt the area around the house was out of alignment. His talisman told him that much. His aching muscles told him it was something he needed to be afraid of. But his head told him the situation was not as impossible as it seemed. By the time he'd joined the others for dinner, he had a Plan B.

But first he had to get through Plan A. Fortunately, Bao had assisted her father on so many occasions she knew the ceremonies by heart and was a patient teacher for Siri. He'd written the various stages of the exorcism on a small cheat sheet and committed some of the more important phrases to memory. He was just about to attempt a full dress rehearsal when they were disturbed by the splutter of tired ponies from outside. The search party had returned.

Siri and Bao hurried outside just as Long and the others emerged from the main house. Dia and Chia were seated on the same horse and behind them, strapped face-down on the second pony, was a rather feral-looking Judge Haeng. He was barely conscious. While the girls unstrapped him Siri looked into his milky eyes and found a weak pulse.

'Did you give him anything to drink?' Siri asked.

'He wouldn't take it from us, Yeh Ming,' Chia told him.

'Or food,' Dia added. 'He just screamed and fainted. Will he live, do you think?'

'I'll be able to get a better look when we get him down from his mount, but I don't see too many problems a little nutrition won't fix. You are excellent trackers. Well done. My heartiest thanks.'

As they helped the judge down, Siri did detect a broken wrist. The fact that there was no cry of pain when Siri grabbed it suggested Haeng had no feeling. The numbness extended to his head. In his stupor he mumbled phrases like, 'What will become of me?' and 'The Lord Buddha protect me,' a plea Siri filed away for some blackmail in the future. Although Long wanted the newcomer to recover in the main house, Siri decided a room to himself would be less traumatic for Haeng if and when he came around. He made up some excuse about the possibility of contagion and they opened up the hut nearest to Siri's own and made it comfortable.

A broken wrist, a lost toenail, several deep lacerations probably caused by running into trees, bruises, a slight fever as a result of malnutrition, and a bad case of poison ivy. But, against all the odds, Judge Haeng would live to tell the tale. Bao looked at his well-manicured fingernails and soft hands.

'He isn't your assistant, is he, Yeh Ming?'

'In fact, he's my chief,' Siri confessed.

'But . . . but he's much younger than you.'

'That's the marvellous thing about communism, Bao. Equal opportunity. Even a man without experience has the chance to run a department.'

'It's a silly system.'

'I'll pass on your views to the prime minister next time I see him.' He tightened a splint and wiped the dribbled water from his patient's chin. 'Now, don't I have some rehearsals to complete?'

They walked slowly to the shaman's house but Bao stopped outside.

'It isn't really equal, is it, Yeh Ming?'

'What's that?'

'Communism. I mean, will the government really give a share of their power to the Hmong who fought with them against us? Will they give them good jobs and high positions in the army? There are still the little mice and the big elephants, aren't there?'

'Yes, my general. There are still mice and elephants. But don't forget the elephants used to be mice, so keep eating your spinach.'

*

It was the morning of the exorcism and everyone but Siri, his patient, and, presumably, the honeymoon couple up on the hill, had gone to the fields. Hmong New Year was a day away and they needed to get the opium tapped beforehand. As in most Hmong communities, opium was a source of medicine and revenue. Only the old bothered to smoke it. It was easy to carry in nuggets and would be their currency on the long journey they faced.

Siri had risen to check the progress of Judge Haeng twice during the night. On the second visit the patient allowed himself to be lifted to a sitting position and was able to swallow a large volume of sugared water. For breakfast, Siri spooned a gruel of pork and rice between the judge's cracked lips. Siri imagined him out there in the jungle not trusting any plant or fruit. Not knowing which roots were safe to eat or which insects gave the most nutrition. He was still delirious but once or twice his eyes wandered into the flight path of Siri's and he smiled. A miracle of sorts.

Siri couldn't begin to imagine how he'd be able to explain all this once the little judge had regained control of his faculties. With luck he'd remain non compos mentis until it was all over and the Hmong were on their way. Siri walked outside with his cup of coffee freshly brewed from beans he'd crushed himself. He marvelled once again at the spectacular scenery all around. How would the Hmong be able to live without it? What had they done that was so terrible to deserve banishment to an alien land? They'd lost the war, so what? Laos had forever engaged in battles with itself. 'Forgive thine enemy,' the Christian Bible said. Too bad the Manifesto didn't include that clause.

The final check: on the three-tiered altar sat the silver alms bowl full of spring water, a pork-fat candle, a saucer of husked rice with a complete egg as its centrepiece, and three porcelain bowls of rice wine, tea, and water to satisfy the finicky tastes of the spirits. In his pouch were the divination horns and puffed maize for his horse, the winged steed that would carry the shaman to the Otherworld. Yet right now that particular beast resembled nothing more than a wonky wooden bench with splinters.

Several threads of pure white unspun cotton ran from the altar over the main crossbeam and down to the frame of the door, giving the guests the feeling they were entering the lair of a giant spider. Siri himself was decked out in black pyjamas. Around his head was a macraméd band that held a hooded mask in place. It was pulled back over his head at present but would be lowered when the ceremony began. On the fingers of his right hand were tiny bells that made him sound like a wind chime whenever he tried to scratch his missing earlobe. On the bench were his dagger and rattle. He could hear the audience milling around outside.

'Are you nervous?' Bao asked him.

'Nervous? Me? Dr Siri Paiboun, the national coroner with a lifetime membership in the communist party? Are you serious? I'm scared witless. I never was much for costume drama. I got terrible stage fright at high school in Paris when they forced me to act. Did I tell you I went to high school in France? They made me repeat everything from eighth grade before they'd let me study medicine. It didn't help that all the costumes were twice my size. I was five years older than everyone else and half as big. They made me look like a little boy playing dress up. I'll never forget— I'm babbling, aren't I?'

'Yes.'

'Sure sign the adrenaline's pumping.'

They heard the excited chatter of the audience coming to the door.

'Oh, my word,' he said.

'Don't worry about it, Yeh Ming. Just go through it the way we did last night. They'll never know.'

He looked into her sparkling eyes.

'How old are you?'

'Eighteen. Why?'

'I sometimes get the feeling you're an old person reincarnated.'

'Old people aren't necessarily that smart, Yeh Ming.'

'*Touché.*'

Siri sat carefully on the winged steed. He nodded solemnly first at Elder Long, who was wearing his best suit for the occasion, then at his three wives. Each was attempting to out-dress the others. Their costumes were evidence of many years of work and great depth of artistic feeling. He smiled at the unattached ladies and waited for them to sit cross-legged in front of their elder's seat. The room was full and Siri thanked the stars that two hundred more guests hadn't been able to make it to the ceremony.

There came an almighty crash that almost bucked him from his horse. It was Bao bringing the house to order with her gong. Siri took a deep breath to restart his heart. Once his assistant had the audience's attention she began to beat the instrument steadily, two heartbeats per gong. Siri composed himself, picked up the ceremonial dagger, and walked to the altar. With a rather impressive flourish, he buried the knife almost to its hilt in the dirt floor. So far, so good. He lit the incense and the foul-smelling candle and returned to the bench. He reached into his pouch and produced the divination horns. These had been cut from the tip of a buffalo horn and split lengthwise to make two similar halves. How the horns landed when cast onto the ground would tell the shaman what particular ailment the elder's daughter was suffering from (although Siri hardly needed horns to tell him that) and how best to go about healing her. He cupped both hands around them, shook them extravagantly like a gambler in Monte Carlo, and threw them onto the ground at his feet.

There was a gasp from the onlookers. Something had gone wrong already. One of the horns had cracked in half down its axis, leaving not two but three divining markers. The newly split horn formed a perfect cross. The unbroken horn landed horizontally beside it. It was symmetrical. No casino would have given odds on it. Siri had no idea what it meant. He was angry he'd shaken the horns too hard but he pretended it was all perfectly normal. He leaned down to study the formation and nodded knowingly. Once satisfied he sat square on the bench and breathed heavily.

This was to be the point at which Bao would lower the hood, but Siri happened to look up at that moment to see a delirious but conscious Judge Haeng leaning against the door frame wearing nothing but a splint and a pair of underpants. He glared drunkenly around the room and seemed to recognize one Dr Siri dressed as a Hmong and riding a wooden horse. Siri shrugged and let the flap drop over his face. One crisis at a time. The show had to go on.

The actual process of getting a shaman into a trance

could have taken an hour or more, but he and Bao had decided fifteen minutes would be sufficient in this particular case. She increased the tempo to one gong stroke per heart-beat. He found that it curiously matched his own pulse so closely it was as if his heart had acquired a sound effect. This in turn reminded him of his own percussion role. He reached beside him for the rattle and began to shake it. He had a surprisingly good sense of rhythm for a septuagenarian. By the time he'd incorporated the finger bells he thought that at another time and place they might even have been able to make a few *kip* playing backup band at temple fairs.

He had to keep track of the timing. The hood had disorientated him but he had to remember to begin his unconscious twitching at about the right time. There was something haunting about the rhythm and he was afraid he'd already forgotten to do something important. What was that? Never mind. As he didn't possess the gift of tongues and he was supposed to yell every now and then, he decided that French would be sufficiently incomprehensible to the audience. Although he found himself forgetting the words and slurring through much of it, he recited the chorus of 'La Marseillaise':

Grab your weapons, citizens!
Form your battalions!
Let us march! Let us march!
May . . . da dee dee da

The gong was beating faster now along with his racing heart and his arm was aching from all the rattling. His head was nodding and his foot was tapping to the beat. He completely forgot whether he was to mount the bench at this time or simply stand and fall back into his assistant's waiting arms. A lot of conflicting thoughts were going through his mind, memories of events that had no place there. His amulet seemed to sizzle against his skin. Feed the horse? Now? He reached into his pouch, grabbed a handful of puffed maize, and threw it into the air, shouting, 'Ride 'em, cowboy,' one of his few English phrases, harvested from a favourite John Wayne movie. For some reason his arm continued to flutter in the air there and he couldn't get it to come down.

He had pins and needles in his legs so when he looked down through the gap beneath his hood he was surprised to see his feet kicking out into thin air. To recall his errant limbs he swung his body a little carelessly over the bench to sit astride his winged steed. He was sure he'd skewered himself on a splinter or two but his bottom was numb as a loaf of bread. During the previous night's rehearsal all the shaking and leaping had tuckered him out after no more than five minutes but he was riding feverishly now and felt nothing at all. 'La Marseillaise' had become complete gibberish even to him and the gong beats blended together and faded away like ink spots in a pond.

And he was gone – a dream – a hallucination – the effects of a wood splinter puncturing an important nerve? He wasn't sure which. But something had sent him. And the place he'd arrived at was more real than the one he'd just left. He felt – not sensed but actually felt – the winged horse between his thighs. He felt and smelled and tasted the night air rushing against his face. The moisture in the clouds they passed through was icy cold on his cheeks. His senses in the real world had been draining of late. There were no distinct colours or tastes in the actual Laos. But they were all here. They assaulted and bombarded him. This was his new reality.

The muscles of his steed flexed and relaxed as the huge white wings found currents of air on which to glide down towards the building tops. Siri's stomach heaved as the creature soared and dove between the skyscrapers. He clung to the cusp of a wing and its force vibrated through him. They flew down past office windows where men in shirts and ties drank coffee and watched them pass with looks of astonishment on their Western faces. Then an apartment building where a woman in curlers hanging washing from her window was so shocked she dropped her stockings and they floated down to the street like wisps of smoke from the tenth storey.

Lower and darker: the smells of smog and fried meat and garbage and hairspray. And a bump. The winged steed skidded to a stop on the icy pavement and white steam smudged the air around her nostrils. Her front hoof scraped at the ground and she shook her mane. Siri stayed put.

'This is the Otherworld?' he asked. For some reason he expected a flying horse would have the ability to speak. 'This is where all the shamans come to negotiate for lost souls? I'm disappointed, I don't mind telling you.'

She didn't answer with words and he didn't speak whinny so he gave up and climbed down. He wasn't appropriately dressed at all. He knew he'd catch his death of cold. He felt the burn of the ice on the soles of his bare feet. Yet instinctively he knew the thrill of it – the warming excitement of being on the other side – would keep him alive. His thudding heartbeat alone could power a tank.

They'd arrived on a deserted main street at the mouth of

a dark alleyway. He looked at the horse, who in turn looked towards the side street.

'I was afraid you'd say that.'

Siri walked into the yawning darkness and immediately felt a morbid sense of familiarity. He'd been here recently. He'd walked along these uneven paving stones and squinted through the gray lamplight. It was his dream. This was the selfsame place he'd walked on the day he was given the sleeping poison. He knew what to expect. He knew that up ahead he'd meet two thugs and be attacked. He stopped. Common sense told him that he should learn from his mistakes. The dream had been a warning. He had no weapon still. He couldn't outrun them.

'No, Siri. Go back to the horse and find a different path. Once bitten . . .'

He turned on his heel and headed back the way he'd come. But the stones seemed more uneven than they had just been. The street lamps stretched further into the distance than was possible. He passed a doorway he hadn't noticed and heard familiar voices from the shadows.

'Well, whaddya know? The gook's back.'

'So he is. What's new, Red? Been busy torturing the good guys, have ya?'

This was wholly different from the dream. It had an extra dimension. In dreams he was in some kind of control, aware that he was in a dream. Even when he was frightened by them, something at the back of his mind told him it would all be over at cockcrow. But this all felt so real. His feet and fingers were aching from the cold. He had a terrible urge to go to the bathroom and a tingle of fear rode the back of his neck. Up ahead, in the direction he thought he'd come from, he saw the lights of the Silver Pheasant.

Somehow, he had to do a better job of getting past these goons.

'Look,' he said. 'If you leave me alone I won't call on my auxiliary spirits.'

'Ooooh,' mocked the first thug, stepping out of the doorway. The lamplight turned his skull the colour of nicotine-stained teeth. He seemed to have grown in stature since they'd last met. Siri considered asking whether he'd been working out but decided it was a bad time for humour.

'You hear that, Eric?' the thug said. 'Grandpa's gonna call the auxes.'

Eric remained in the shadows.

'Think you might be too late, Red Man,' the second thug said.

Siri knew the skeleton was right. That was what he'd forgotten. He could see it underlined on his cheat sheet. 'Must invoke guiding spirits *before* going into trance.' He was a hopeless shaman. But, hell, he hadn't planned all this. It was supposed to be a hoax. It was worth a try anyway.

'I'm warning you,' he said.

'I'm trembling,' said the first thug.

'Very well.' Like some ancient magician, Siri raised his arms to the tops of the buildings that towered over him. 'I invoke the spirit of the otter.'

'Tsk tsk,' came a sound from the shadows. 'Did he invoke the otter, Danny?'

'Sure did, Eric.'

'Bad choice, Reddo. You should have gone for the eagle.'

'Much better idea, gook. Otters are for water problems and what you've got' – Eric stepped out of the doorway, almost twice his previous size – 'is mugger problems.'

'Go through his pockets while he's still standing, Danny boy.'

The first goon had a solid presence about him, like a front-end loader with attitude. Siri had no pockets but he allowed the pouch to be plucked from his waist without any retaliation.

'Then I invoke the spirit of the great eagle,' Siri said, half-heartedly. Nothing happened.

'Give it up, Red Man.'

'Don't you listen, gook?' Eric said, leaning against the wall with a Lucky Strike dangling unlit from his lower jaw. He was even more stained and chipped than his colleague. 'You've blown it. You gotta invoke before you get on the horse, man.' He leaned down into Siri's face and breathed rotten teeth at him. 'You're aux-less.'

The first thug was digging down through the pouch, throwing out puffed maize.

'He got any money?' Eric asked.

'Nah, nothing.'

'Shit, let's kill him.'

'No wait.' The thug known as Danny had found something deep in the pouch. 'Oh, man, look!'

His hand emerged from the bag with two bone fingers holding onto a button. Siri had forgotten all about it, didn't even recall putting it in the pouch. It was the button he'd dredged up from the bottom of the rock pool. Danny handed it to Eric, who looked at Siri with as much emotion as a skull could ever hope to muster.

'So he knows.' Eric nodded.

'Looks like it.'

'Have to let him go.'

'I guess.'

'You owe us for this, gook.'

'Big-time.'

Eric flipped the button into the air like a coin. Siri glanced up for a second and caught it on its way back down. But when he turned his head towards the muggers, they were no longer there. He looked around and he was all alone in that badly lit place.

'Most peculiar,' he thought.

He looked at the button. There was nothing special about it: green plastic, normal size for a shirt. He held it to his nose to see whether his enhanced sense of smell might tell him something. It had been submerged in water so he didn't hold out much hope, but there was a very faint scent of . . . desperation.

'Remember where you are, Siri. Remember, none of this is credible.'

He put the button back in his pouch and staggered forward over the uneven stones to the end – or the beginning – of the alley. On the far side of a busy boulevard the gaudy lights of the Silver Pheasant beckoned. He negotiated the traffic with no problem as it was without substance, blurs of metallic paint flying past in either direction. But on the far pavement he encountered a long queue of shamans dressed much like he was, all waiting to get into the club. A huge black bouncer stood at the door with a list in his hand and a pistol sticking out of his belt. As Siri didn't consider himself to have any special rights over the others, he nodded and smiled at the waiting men and women and joined the back of the line.

Four hours later he was still there and the queue hadn't advanced more than a step or two. Others had fallen in behind him but none of his line mates seemed particularly talkative. He kept himself entertained by singing the Hmong refrain to the dead he'd learned at the funeral.

Aha, your ghost, my sister, richly dressed
Appears on the other side,
Pretty like you – your spitting image
Is it you or not?
Look, that woman, that stranger,
She sings you a spirit song,
Your ghost takes you by the hand and—

His song was interrupted by a big booming voice from up ahead.

'Yeh Ming, is that you, man?'

Siri looked up to see the bouncer on the pavement looking over the heads of the other shamans. He held his knuckles against his waist and wore a big gappy grand-piano smile across his mouth.

'I don't believe it,' he said. 'It is too.'

He waded into the crowd like a whale through sardines and hugged Siri to him so tightly that Siri would carry the indentation of a pistol on his stomach for days.

'You son of a gun,' the bouncer continued. He took a step back and looked at Siri's confused face. 'Don't you recognize me, Yeh Ming? It's me, man. See Yee.'

Siri racked his brains. The only See Yee he could recall was the first Hmong shaman, a sort of god of shamans. He'd always imagined him to be more . . . well, this wasn't the way he'd imagined him to look.

'Good health,' Siri said.

'Good health? Good health is all I get after all them years? After all we been through, Yeh Ming?'

'You're right, sorry.'

'You must be— What you doing back here in the queue anyhow? You're Yeh Ming. Get your boney little fanny up front.'

There were groans and complaints from the assembled shamans.

'Come on! I was here first.'

'I've been here a month.'

'I'm telling my local representative. This isn't the way we . . .'

'Hey, cool it, guys,' See Yee said, leading Siri to the main door. 'This here is Yeh Ming. You guys gotta do a helluva lot of standing before you're even nearly worthy of kissing this shaman's behind. So shut your whining.'

With a wink, he ushered Siri through the doors and told him they'd catch up later. It took Siri a moment to get used to the glare inside. He'd been expecting some type of club – disco music and the like, crowds of dancing shamans and the stale smell of beer. What he saw in fact was a huge open-air swimming pool, even bigger than Olympic size. In the water, floating on an inflatable raft, was a little man with a pot belly and a martini glass. His sunglasses were so large it was impossible to tell his ethnicity. Beneath the surface all around him were large green lizard-like creatures. They performed in pairs like synchronized swimmers.

At the side of the pool, under an enormous purple beach umbrella, was a wooden desk piled high with papers and folders and alphabetically indexed ledgers. Siri's wave to the man in the pool went unanswered so he approached the desk. Even a few feet away it was impossible to tell whether there was anyone in residence. Not till he heard the voice.

'Name?'

Siri tried to look around the stacks but saw no one.

'Dr Siri Paiboun,' he said.

There was a brief flutter of papers.

'Don't have anyone here with such a name. Next!' said the voice.

Siri walked around to the side of the desk and peered through the folders. He could only see a crop of ginger hair above the piles.

'I'm here to negotiate for the soul of a friend's daughter,' Siri said.

'Oh, really? And I thought you might be here to fix the filter system,' the voice said impatiently. 'Next!'

'Well, I could have a look at it for you,' Siri said. 'But I'm better with water pumps.'

He heard a nasal huff.

'It was sarcasm, brother. All we do here is negotiate for souls. But we don't have any daughters on our lists called Dr Siri Paiboun. Now, if you don't mind . . .'

'Oh, I see. Her name isn't Dr Siri Paiboun.'

'So why did you say it was?'

Siri pushed over a stack of files with his finger. It collapsed a second and a third stack and exposed a stunned, red-faced man who looked at him through bloodshot eyes.

'Wh . . . ?'

Siri said, 'You find some of the most bad-mannered people in jobs dealing with the public. Why do you suppose that is?'

'What?'

'It takes skills to deal with people day in and day out. Customers have feelings, you know? It isn't that difficult to show a little courtesy and civility. It takes no more effort to make your clients happy than it does to depress the socks off them. If you can't do that, I don't really know why you're here. There are plenty of noncontact careers available for bookkeepers.'

There was a long silence during which the two stared at each other. The ginger-haired man swallowed and his voice broke a little as he said, 'I'm Nyuwa Tuatay, the deputy overlord of the Otherworld.'

'Then, as I say, perhaps you should be looking for a position that better suits your personality. And who's he?' Siri asked, pointing to the figure on the air mattress.

'You don't know?'

'Would I ask if I did?'

'That is Nyuwa Neyu, the great overlord.'

'I'd say you drew the short straw, comrade.'

The man in the pool smiled and beckoned Siri to join him.

'Sorry, I can't swim. Perhaps next time.'

Another silence.

'What can I do for you?' the bookkeeper asked.

'Much better. I'm here to negotiate for the soul of a friend's daughter.'

'And her name is?' He added, 'If you'd be so kind.'

Siri smiled. 'Chamee Mua.'

'Age?'

'Fourteen.'

There was more flipping of pages. Siri looked over at the pool. A blonde nymph in a polka dot bikini was swimming out with a fresh martini. Being the overlord of the Otherworld didn't seem to be the most taxing of jobs. He considered taking an application form himself.

'I'm sorry,' Nyuwa Tuatay told Siri.

'What's wrong?'

'I don't have a Chamee Mua on my list . . . and I've checked twice.'

'And what does that mean?'

'It probably means all her souls are still with her.'

Siri stepped out of the sun and into the shade of the umbrella to consider matters.

'Hmm,' he said.

'Anything else I can do?' the deputy asked respectfully.

'What if she were possessed by a demon?' Siri asked.

'Oh, then that's a different department altogether.'

'And that is?'

'Demons reside in the Land of the Dead.'

'And how do I get there?'

'You die.'

'Really? I can't just go and visit?'

'Can a tree in the forest temporarily fall down?'

'Is that a "no"?'

'It is.'

Siri walked a slow circuit of the desk and came back to the clearing he'd forged through the paperwork.

'One more question,' he said.

'Please.'

'If a person were possessed by a devil, isn't it likely his or her soul would be troubled and you'd have some record?'

'One would think so. But I'm not qualified to do philosophy here,' the deputy told him matter-of-factly. 'That's two blocks east on Seventy-fifth. Here's their card.'

Siri knew he had a room full of people waiting for him back on earth but he spent some time chewing the fat with See Yee on the front step, talking about old times he wasn't personally a part of, before heading back towards the alley.

He didn't bother with the Philosophy Department. He already had his answer. The winged steed was parked on the main street at the far end of the walkway where he'd left it. A traffic warden was looking for somewhere to attach a ticket. Siri ignored him, climbed majestically onto the horse's back, and flew away.

There was a splinter in Siri's backside. He felt it as he fell backward into Bao's waiting arms. She was a deceptively strong girl.

'OK, Yeh Ming. That should do,' she whispered so only he could hear. She pulled back the mask and the afternoon sun through the window blinded him. He was surprised it was still day. He continued to sit astride the bench. The rattle was no longer in his hand. The audience remained remarkably enthralled considering the number of hours he'd been away. Elder Long looked at Siri with admiration: the great Yeh Ming presiding over an exorcism right here in his own village. Who would have believed it? He nodded his head and raised his eyebrows as if expecting Siri to give him a summary of the trip.

Siri was far from certain what had just happened.

'I need a while to prepare my report,' Siri said.

Nobody in the room moved.

'Alone,' he added. Long and the women got to their feet and paraded out the door. When they were gone and only he and Bao remained in the shaman's hut he whispered excitedly, 'I did it.'

'It was quite convincing,' she said, putting out the candle. 'You were better in the rehearsal but I expect you were nervous.'

'No, I mean I did it. I went to the Otherworld.'

She turned to him. 'Yeh Ming, there are just the two of us here.'

'I know. So I have no reason to lie.'

She walked to him and knelt by the bench. 'You're serious, Yeh Ming.'

'I am. I can hardly believe it myself. If I was anybody else I'd call me a liar too. Isn't it marvellous?'

'Tell me about it. Tell me everything.'

'Well, I was rather expecting caves and an underground lake and a mountain, all the things I'd read in the legends.'

'My father said the location can depend on influence from the victim and the imagination of the shaman.'

'Is that so? Then I have no idea who's been playing with my head.'

'Where were you?'

'Somewhere in North America, I believe. It was a city. Nowhere I've ever been in real life. There were skyscrapers and the streets had a layer of ice.'

Siri told her the whole story. There were parts that neither of them understood – the street thugs foremost among them – but everything else was as logical as necromancy can be.

'And all that in three hundred heartbeats. Wonderful.' Bao smiled.

'Three hundred? Why that's not much more than five minutes. I was only in the trance for five minutes?'

'At the most. You've done very well, Yeh Ming. I'm happy for you. But I'm sad for Elder Long.'

'Why?'

'You learned nothing about Chamee.'

'Oh, but I did.'

'I don't understand.'

'You will. But first I have to go to her house again.'

'Are you sure? You still have the bruises from last time.'

'Ah, but last time I didn't know what I was dealing with.' He stood and gently patted his rear end.

'And now you do?'

'I hope so.'

'I'll come with you.'

'No, Bao. Not this time. This is something I have to do by myself. It'll be all right. I promise.'

'I trust you.'

Siri retrieved the ceremonial dagger from the earth and used the rice whisky to clean the earth from it.

'I should think this is pretty well sanctified now, wouldn't you?'

He walked gingerly to the door but stopped as he reached the doorway. An unpleasant memory had suddenly returned to him.

'Did you happen to see . . . ?'

'Your weak-minded "assistant"? He fainted. Dia took him back to his bed.'

'Do you think he'll remember?'

'I'm afraid he might.'

'Damn.'

13

SIRI CONFRONTS HIS DEMON

Siri walked uncomfortably up the trail past the blackened stumps until he reached the first bush. He ducked behind it and checked back to be sure he wasn't being followed. Once he was certain he was alone, he carefully lowered his trousers to his ankles and inspected his bottom. There were two fairly large splinters, neither one of which he could see. But they were protruding enough for him not to have need of the knife. He gritted his teeth and yanked them free. Bao had probably seen worse but this operation was hardly something to be done in front of a lady. She was really quite a remarkable girl. There was something of his ex-wife, Boua, about her, that same determination and . . .

He slapped himself on the forehead. Such thoughts didn't help anyone. His wounds smarted when he pulled up his pyjama bottom. He'd have to find some antiseptic, but later. He had a demon to confront.

He approached the house quietly although there was little need. Chamee's screams coming from inside were loud enough to raise the dead. There was no time for caution. He hoped he could catch the demon by surprise. He hurdled the re-erected lattice fence but avoided the front path. He crashed through the land bridges, sending their parts flying all around. He fought his way through the branches and nettles at one side of the house and arrived at an open window. The first thing he noticed was the blood. It seemed to be everywhere. Chamee was sitting naked on the dirt floor, her back against the centre pillar, her legs akimbo. She was ghostly white and covered in blood and sweat . . . and *he* was standing over her.

Everyone in the village seemed to hear the screams at the same time. They came rushing from the main house, and, without speaking, converged on the pathway. Each of them carried a weapon of some kind: machetes, muskets, crossbows, knives. And they ran like the spirits of the wind up the mountain. Even old Long found the energy to remain not a few paces behind them. They reached the lattice fence and stared at the now-silent house. The front door was closed and Siri was nowhere to be seen. Long joined the others just as another scream rent the air. Birds fled their nests and took to the sky. Long put a foot forward but Nhia grabbed his arm.

'We have to help her,' he said.

'You know we can't,' Nhia told him. 'Even Yeh Ming couldn't compete with the force of the demon.'

'I can't just leave her in there, suffering,' Long told her and wrestled his arm free. He began to move forward but now Bao and one or two others held him back.

'No, Elder Long,' Bao said. 'I'll go.'

The others argued with her, begged her not to try. They reminded her what had happened the first time she'd attempted to enter the house. There came another scream. Bao took a breath and marched to the fence. As Siri had done before, she worked loose the post and let the latticework fall to the ground. She stepped over it and raised her machete above her head. She planned to charge the door.

'Stop,' came a voice from inside. She looked up to see the door slightly ajar now and Siri, exhausted, peering through the gap. 'It's dangerous here. Go back beyond the fence. You can't help. Just wait.'

Bao could see his hand on the door. It was covered in blood.

'Yeh Ming, you're hurt,' she cried.

'It's nothing serious. Please . . . please.'

She stepped back over the fence and joined the others. The door closed and there was silence. Until the next scream.

That was the scream that woke Judge Haeng. He recalled having woken before, being fed water and gruel. There had been nightmares and fantastic dreams. He thought perhaps he'd left his bed once and seen . . . or perhaps not. He looked around at his surroundings. A pagan hut. Was he a prisoner? There were no chains. A guard outside?

'I'm hungry,' he called in a hoarse voice. 'Do you plan to feed me?'

But there was no response. In fact, the door was open. Small ugly black pigs sniffed around him. He tried to sit up. His head was foggy. His stomach felt nauseous. But he could sit. That was when he noticed his splint and the bandages and the foul-smelling balm on his skin. A hospital, that's what it was. He'd been rescued. It *was* Siri he'd seen at his bedside.

'Hello,' he called. 'I'm hungry.' Still nobody came.

He got to his feet, found his balance, kicked a mangy long-haired mutt out of his way, and staggered to the door. A village. He was in a pagan village in the middle of damned nowhere. Deserted all but for some stunted horses and a few other mindless animals. He had to learn to walk on his legs. He wobbled to the nearest hut. Some animist shrine there with . . . a what? A toy in the middle? How would these people ever become civilized when here they were worshipping toys?

His nose led him in the direction of food. There was certainly something cooking in the largest hut. It took him some time to get there but his stomach rallied his legs forward. Nobody in the main hut either but a huge pot sat slow-boiling over embers. He grabbed a cloth and lifted the lid. It wasn't French cuisine but it appeared to have some nutritional value. He washed his hands in a tub of water, took a bowl, and scooped it into the soup. He took a spoon, sat on a bamboo ledge, and ate heartily.

If he'd been in less of a hurry, he might have found the pot of gruel cooking on the stove hearth. That was for humans. The larger pot was kept boiling throughout the day. It was for the pigs. Anything unfit for human consumption found its way into that pot: the left over, the inedible, the unpleasant and indescribable. They all ended up in the pig swill. The Hmong believed that if you kept that mish-mash boiling long enough, the livestock wouldn't know it from food.

Three hours had passed and barely a word had been exchanged by the onlookers. Flies had found their way to the blood and the house buzzed with their presence like badly wired telegraph lines. A heavy black crow sat observing from a nearby stump. The screaming had stopped some time before but the silence was, in many ways, worse. Left to their own imaginations, terrible thoughts passed through the heads of Long and the women. They visualized

Yeh Ming's battle with the demon. Saw him being too late to stop the sacrifice. And even now they knew not whether their great shaman had survived. He had instructed them to wait, so wait they did. But for how long? What if Yeh Ming lay wounded inside and in need of help?

The door suddenly swung open as if of its own volition, as if gasping for air. The mouths of the viewers mirrored its gape. Seconds passed, then minutes, and there was no movement and no sound. Even the crow sat spellbound. And finally, Dr Siri, their own Yeh Ming, emerged from the house with an exhausted smile on his lips. And in each arm he carried a bonny round baby. He walked unhindered through the tunnel of vines, crossed the lattice fence, and stood facing Long.

'Congratulations,' he said. 'You're a grandfather.'

The women, still carrying their mental images of terror, approached the babies cautiously. Did they sport horns? Have fangs? Did they have all the requisite limbs and organs?

'Are they . . . ?' Long began.

'They're perfectly normal, perfectly healthy human beings,' Siri smiled. Although they were certainly pretty babies, he didn't add the word 'beautiful' in case the infant-stealing *dab* spirits were listening.

Long beamed with pride and took one of the babies in his arms. Chia took the other and the women flocked around them, cooing at their prettiness. Bao stepped forward and threw her arms around Siri as if some unspoken prayer had been answered. It was an ecstatic and awkward moment that lasted all of four heartbeats.

'And Chamee?' Long asked. 'Where is my daughter?'

It was the question Siri had dreaded. He pulled away

from Bao and stood before Long with his hands clasped in front of him. He shook his head.

'I'm afraid it was too much for her,' he said.

The elation subsided suddenly. Yet, if they were to be honest with themselves, they'd all long given up hope of Chamee's surviving this. Once the devil had her body, their only hope had been that they might retrieve her soul.

'How did she . . . ?' Long began.

'It's something that shouldn't be spoken of,' Siri replied. Bao looked at him with surprise.

'You have to understand that,' he continued. 'All you need to know is that the demon didn't get her soul or those of her children. Before she . . . went, she'd seen the girls and she knew she was free. She could never have been happier. She told me she would take her love for you all to the Land of the Dead.'

Long nodded slowly as he considered the alternatives and seemed to come to a conclusion. He had lost his daughter but she had died content and free of possession. And in her stead he had two beautiful grandchildren. Yes, he could live with that. There was only one more matter. He looked at the house and Siri pre-empted the inevitable question. With one of the babies still squirming against his chest, he led the old man away from the flock and put his arm on his shoulder.

'Long, there cannot be a traditional burial.'

'But . . .'

Siri knew Long would struggle with such a possibility but Yeh Ming had already warned the elder not to speak of events and he knew better than to go against such a directive.

'All the arrangements have been made,' Siri told him.

'When the time is right, Chamee will travel to the Land of the Dead and be reincarnated. You know who I am and how much influence I have. To prevent this happening again, that house and all it contains must be destroyed as it is.'

Again there was a look of horror on Long's face. Questions gathered behind it, questions he could not ask. The baby gurgled and its face puckered into a near smile and Long resolved to accept Yeh Ming's decision.

'So be it, Yeh Ming.'

When he ordered the women to torch the house they were shocked. One or two even ventured to question him.

'You're sure this is the only way?' Nhia asked calmly.

'Yes,' he replied.

One look at the faces of the two old men told them that there was no discussion to be had. A decision had been made and they had to trust that it was the correct one.

Nobody could abide to sit and watch the house burn. They'd returned to the village, all of them, and were busying themselves with preparations for their departure. Nothing could keep them there now. General Bao had gone to her father's hut, retrieved a quart of paraffin and a Zippo, and walked back up to the house. As per Siri's instructions, she had avoided entering the cursed place and set her fire against the front wall. It was an old building and it accepted the flames with an unnatural hunger. Even before the villagers reached the village the explosions had begun. They all tried to ignore the violent conflagration that rose in a storm from the evil house. No fire had ever displayed such colours or emitted a blacker smoke. No fire had ever crashed and blasted heavenward with such intensity. They tried their hardest not to stare at the mountaintop but it was a spectacular inferno and they knew it would attract attention from many kilometres away. Their departure could not be too soon.

When they'd first returned to the village, Long and the women had found Yeh Ming's feeble-minded "assistant" wracked with pain and curled on the ground in front of the main house. His stomach growled like a dying dog. Pigs circled around him, land vultures awaiting his final breath. At first the women assumed it was part of the exorcism, the assistant reliving the pain of the master, but Siri arrived, saw the half-eaten pig swill, and diagnosed the condition as chronic food poisoning. What he couldn't explain was what had turned the judge's hands nearly black. It gave the appearance that Haeng was rotting from the fingers up. This mystery was solved by Ber, who pointed to the tub of indigo they used to dye their cloth. It would appear the judge had washed his hands in it before attempting to poison himself.

They rushed him back to his hut and Siri performed a tried and tested form of bush stomach pumping involving a length of hose and a football bladder. He hoped it would have the desired effect but, by then, he was so exhausted he didn't really care. If Haeng was so intent on killing himself, who was Siri to intervene? The judge's black gloves brought a smile to Siri's face before he returned to the shaman's hut. The cacophony of sound from the old house on the hilltop had ceased but the sky all around was dirty with its ghost. He was pleased it was all over but he needed sleep. This day seemed to have been endless, so full of lies and deceit he barely deserved to wake up. He crawled onto the bamboo platform and his battered bones clacked as they settled. The last image that burned itself on his pupils was of the sun still squeezing through the bamboo slats. After all he'd been through that day, how could it not be night?

It was truly night when he awoke to feel the knife blade at his neck. The pig-fat candle burned on the altar but there was no other light. The shadow of his attacker loomed black against the candlelight.

'Had enough sleep?' He heard and smelled the sweet earthiness of rice wine.

'Are you really planning to cut my throat?' he asked. 'After all I've been through?'

'I might.'

'And what's my crime?' He was barely awake and still heavy with exhaustion.

'Lying.'

'You're drunk.'

'And why shouldn't I be?' Bao asked. Even though her knife rode his Adam's apple, her young breasts were pressed against his arm as she lay beside him. He could feel her breaths, heavy and fast as a boxer's at the bell. 'Everything I know and love will be gone in the morning.'

'For goodness' sake, take that blade away. You might do some damage.'

'I intend to. It's my plan to cut out your lying tongue, great Yeh Ming.' She sighed and rolled onto her back. The knife went with her. Siri sidled away and propped himself up on one elbow.

'You're going in the morning?'

'Everything's done here so we'll join the big march tomorrow. Tonight's our farewell party. I've been sent to wake you and drag you to it.'

'Then let's go.'

'Not yet. First I have to . . .'

'Cut out my tongue. I know. But I can't imagine why you'd want to.'

'Don't!' The knife returned and this time there might have been a slight nick. She was very drunk and the words left her mouth angrily and badly pronounced. 'Don't make fun of me.'

'I'm not. You don't know what you're saying. You've had too much—'

She sat up and stabbed the knife into the sleeping platform. Its blade reflected the flicker of the candle.

'I know I'm drunk. It's temporary. So don't talk to me like one of the addicts behind the Phonsavan market. Tomorrow I'll be sober but I won't recover from your humiliation if you keep lying to me. I need to know what happened up there, and don't give me the demon . . . unspoken . . . cremation shit. Show me some respect.'

Siri saw the fire in her beautiful eyes and fell deeply in love with her. He swung his legs off the platform and felt the pain of his splinter wounds. He sat for a moment staring at the ground. She remained silent beside him.

'If I tell you,' he said, 'you have to swear to me on the souls of your ancestors that you won't tell Elder Long or the others. And I mean now and for ever.'

'Is it so terrible?'

'Promise!'

'All right.'

'Say the words.'

'I swear not to tell.' She pulled her legs under her and sat cross-legged on the platform. Siri chose to stand to tell his tale, prancing back and forth.

'I'm a cynic,' he began, 'albeit a cynic who is constantly confounded by the truth. I have to be convinced before I believe. When a man tells me in theory it's possible to examine the genetic make-up of blood to identify a killer, I ask to see it in practice so I can believe it. That's why I shall never become a better surgeon while I'm stuck in this country. When a man tells me the world will improve if everyone works together and shares its wealth, I may appreciate the theory but I expect evidence, some proof that man is capable of such selflessness. That's why I'm such a poor communist.

'So when I'm told a demon has assaulted a village girl I need to see evidence that such a thing is possible. Getting zapped in the front yard was quite convincing and the fact that she carried a baby the size of a small buffalo was impressive. But I have to eliminate the other possibilities and be left with only one, that she was impregnated by a demon. I consider how else these feats could be arrived at.

'My biggest problem as a practising cynic, however, is that I'm aligned, against my will and better judgment, to another world. I'm connected to a world of spirits and souls and gods and no matter how hard I try to disprove this world, I know it exists. I don't know how it's possible, but, damn it, it's there. So I resort to the rules of the supernatural. I begin by seeing whether the incredible can be explained through their rules. And when that world tells me something is off-kilter and implausible, I know I have to think as a human. I have to use logic. My visit to the Otherworld told me I had to look for earthly solutions to this mystery.

'The only reason I didn't fathom what really happened to me was that we're in the middle of nowhere in a village without power. But it should have been obvious when I saw the burn marks and bruises. I just couldn't imagine how anyone could get a generator all the way up here or have the wherewithal to set up a system. But I recalled hearing a roar from the house and I wondered whether that might have been a generator sound. And the possibility that this was some elaborate trick entered my mind. If that was so, Chamee had to be a party to it. What I got when I walked to the haunted house wasn't a bolt from the blue, it was an electric shock. The reading of the horns should have told me, the positive and negative charges. Do you know much about electricity?'

'Only what I've seen in the city. Not enough.'

Siri's meanderings were now taking him in wide circles around Bao. The breeze from his body fanned the candle every time he passed.

'Well, I asked myself how a young village girl would have the knowledge and access to equipment to be able to set this up. I hypothesized that she had to have an accomplice. Who, I wondered, would know about electronics and mechanics?'

'A soldier,' Bao filled in.

'Right. And why would a soldier be secretly holed up in a house, afraid to be seen? And why would Chamee go along with it?'

Siri gave Bao a few seconds to consider this.

'A deserter,' she said at last, 'and a lover. One of our own who had come home on leave one time.'

'And?'

'And made her pregnant.'

The turning over of Bao's mind had cleared her whiskied head. She was fully alert now and able to join in Siri's logic.

'But no, Yeh Ming. There isn't shame in that,' she said. 'Our young people aren't discouraged from having sex, and accidents happen.'

Siri stopped his pacing and waited for her to arrive at the same conclusion he'd reached. She talked it through with herself.

'Why should they go to so much trouble to hide the truth?' she asked herself. 'What could have possibly forced them to set up such a complicated lie? Unless . . .'

'Yes!'

'Oh my lord. They share a family name. They're from the same clan.'

She had hit the nail squarely on the head. The ultimate Hmong taboo. Two people of the same surname could not have carnal knowledge. Even if they knew of no living family connections, that tie, traced all the way back through the legends to the beginning of time, still barred intimacy within the same bloodline. It was a rule as rigid as if the couple were full brother and sister and it carried the same stigma that such a relationship would hold in the West. Any couple who ignored this taboo and their children after them would be despised and ostracized.

'Who was the boy?' she asked.

'I don't think it would help anybody to know that. All you need to understand is that he was not much more than a child himself. When I arrived at the house yesterday he was in a terrible state. The girl's time had come and she was bleeding badly. The babies were too much for her. Not only were they large children but there were two of them. Neither she nor the boy had any idea what to do. She couldn't possibly have birthed the babies by herself. I had to cut them out.'

'And Chamee didn't survive this.'

Siri was silent.

'She did? She's alive?'

'She is.'

'You lied to Elder Long.'

'Not exactly. He heard what he wanted to hear. I merely told him Chamee was no longer there.'

'But how were you able to help her? You had no equipment, no medicine.'

'Ah, but I did.'

'I saw you go up the hill. You had nothing with you.'

'I had the ceremonial knife. That was a good start.'

'A start? What do you mean?'

'Do you remember your father telling you about the bad spirit beyond the mountain-top?'

'Nobody goes there. It is too steep for farming and my father told us there were evil spirits living there. We didn't dare explore.'

'Well, he was right. About ten years ago, at the height of the bombing, a plane went down in that valley. It was before your people moved here to this mountain. It crashed into the gully just beyond the peak. The trees had fallen inward on top of it so it wasn't visible from the air. That's why the pilots and their cargo were never recovered. It was a transporter, not a fighter, so it was full of equipment. Chamee's boyfriend discovered it while he was out foraging. It was stocked with canned food.'

'That's why she didn't need the meals we made for her.'

'They could have eaten for a year.'

'It all makes sense.'

'There was electrical equipment and medical supplies too. They had antiseptic and sterilized dressings and stitching thread. The boy had brought it all up to the house to prepare for the birth. It's true he had no idea what to do with most of it. She was lucky. Even if she'd somehow survived the birth I don't see how she could have raised two babies. She's a baby herself.'

'So . . . ?'

'I convinced her they would be better taken care of by the older women. She seemed relieved in a way. We took her down to the plane to recuperate. I believe the burden of being a mother might have been more than she could take. Without family support I couldn't envisage the couple surviving with two babies. The boy was one heck of an electrician, though. He'd trained as an aircraft mechanic with the Americans. Some technician had taught him all he knew about electronics. The boy had it all set up there in the house. He'd run some wires from a generator to the trees above the path. He'd threaded a few dozen uninsulated wires down through the vines with the ends exposed. All he had to do was adjust the current with a rheostat to— You don't know what I'm talking about, do you?'

'Not a word. But I get the point. What about the voice? That was the boy?'

'With a little help from an ampli— from a machine that makes sound louder. He'd whisper what he was about to say and she'd mime it.'

Bao shook her head. 'I can't believe how deceitful she was. Even before the baby started to show, Chamee told her father of nightmares and demons, of visits to the Otherworld in her dreams. She planted the seeds in his head back then. Long wouldn't have thought for a second that his good daughter had broken her promise to her parents not to go with a boy. He was so certain she was a virgin, the only possible explanation was that she'd been possessed.

'He desperately wanted a shaman to come here to release her but travelling between villages was hard after the changeover. Her belly grew so fast and so big we were sure she'd burst if we didn't get some help. Chamee moved up to the old cottage one night and all these signs started to prove she was really possessed. When I tried to go in and get her I got that same electric shock as you. We'd given up on her. That's when the guides told us Yeh Ming was on the PL side and that you'd be passing through Xiang Khouang. It was like a miracle. Long had told us stories about you – about Yeh Ming – when we were little.'

'I doubt whether—'

They were interrupted by a very drunk Long who fell in through the doorway like a felled fence post. He lay with his face on the earthen floor, laughing. Siri and Bao helped him to his feet.

'Now what – as if I didn't know – were you two up to in here all by yourselves?'

'We weren't . . .' Siri blushed.

'Nah, don't deny it. If I didn't have three wives myself . . .' He laughed. 'But there's plenty of time for that old hanky-panky. You!' – he grabbed Siri's arm – 'Are our guest of honour. We need you.'

He dragged Siri out into the moonlight with Bao tripping happily behind. They were halfway to the main house when it occurred to Long he should relieve himself. Despite the abundance of nature all around them, he walked unsteadily to the latrine, saying something about 'order' and 'discipline.' He instructed Siri to stay where he was. Bao joined him.

'Last question before we get too drunk to care,' she said. 'The house. Why did you order us to burn it?'

'There was ammunition, flares, some kind of defoliant, and a few guns in there. The boy had carried them up from the plane in case they needed to defend themselves. From an entire army by the looks of it. If our rescue party ever makes it here and discovers you have a stash of American arms in your village, you'd be classified as rebels. They'd double the troops out after you and they'd have an excuse to shoot the lot of you on sight, irrespective of whether you were women or old folks. Goodness knows it's going to be hard enough for you to get away without that.'

She kissed him on the cheek. 'Thank you,' she said.

'Didn't I tell you to pack that in?' Long shouted, returning from his business. He staggered into them and held onto their waists. 'And what about your weak-minded assistant?' he asked. 'Do you think we should invite him along to our party too?'

'Ooh, I don't think he'll be awake until at least tomorrow,' Bao told him with a slightly guilty look on her face.

'Now what have you done to him?' Siri asked, not really caring.

'You remember when we first met?'

'The sleeping poison?'

'It was for his own safety. It seems whenever he's conscious he gets himself into trouble.'

'I couldn't agree more,' Siri laughed.

They strode into the main house. Candles and lamps burned everywhere, giving the building a warm and jolly feeling it hadn't known since Yeh Ming's arrival. Dia played the *geng* with so much love the music seemed to throw its arms around the newcomers when they entered. Phia and Ber danced to some entirely different music only the two of them could hear. Despite the comparative youth of the evening, Chia had already collapsed in front of the family altar like an offering and was snoring contentedly. As was her way, she would wake refreshed in a few minutes and start all over again. Zhong's reincarnated father lay on his back cycling his legs through the air.

New senior wife Nhia collected her husband at the door and steered him to his place at the feast. The village's entire stock of rice whisky filled a twenty-gallon drum. They wouldn't be taking it with them so they had no choice but to finish it tonight. There was more roast pork than a man could get through in a lifetime and the vegetable garden had been pillaged. Only the house spirits were down. They moped in the beams and rafters like spoiled children. They knew this was their last night of life after death. Like the Hmong they protected, they had nowhere to go.

14

A MOMENT FROZEN IN COTTON

Siri awoke with the type of head a man who drinks half a barrel of rough rice liquor deserves. His mouth was as dry as the average skeleton's eye socket. He tried to swallow and his windpipe constricted the way an empty balloon might if you sucked instead of blew. His old heart quivered and his bladder felt solid as a bowling ball. If ever Laos were to establish a temperance league he felt sure he could be its poster boy. He rolled painfully onto his back. Something was missing from the collage of life around him. The sun was sawing through the loose thatch, which meant the morning mist had already burned off and he'd overslept. That led him to the conclusion that he'd probably reneged on his promise to help with the morning chores.

He eased his neck against the crick and once more reached to scratch the absent earlobe. That's when he noticed the cloth beside him on the platform. It was the most beautifully embroidered *pa n'tow* he had ever seen. He held it up in front of his face. It was a handcrafted picture on blue/grey cloth no more than eighteen inches square but months of work had gone into its sewing. He held it to his nose and could smell the familiar natural scent of its maker. Bao hadn't struck him as the embroidering type but he knew the skill would have been passed down from her grandmother and mother when she was a little girl. She had learned her lesson beautifully.

He studied the frieze, a photographic moment from the village. There were the houses, the ponies, and the livestock. The spring pond lay in white lines on the hill and wild animals came to drink from it. Women milled around the village in their fine costumes, one swollen with child. Young folk played and men worked. Elder Long and his departed wife, Zhong, stood proudly at its centre holding hands. And, almost as an afterthought, a cloud floated across the sky and on it sat an old man with green eyes and white hair. Above his head, a ring of yellow thread made a halo.

Siri lay back and smiled at his gift, he traced the raised cotton of Bao's needlecraft, and he fancied he smelled her there too on his pillow. Only then did it occur to him what was missing from the village – sound. An unexplained anxiety fell over him. He looked towards the shaman's altar. The pogo stick and all its trappings were gone. He forgot his aches and pains and made for the door. Once his eyes were accustomed to the bright sunlight he was able to look about him at the empty village. There were no animals. The chicken coop and stable were empty. No surviving pigs, no goats, no reincarnated dogs. And no people.

He hurried across the compound to the main house and stood in the doorway. The room partitions were disassembled and the dirt floor had been excavated here and there: one hole beneath the central beam where once the placentas of all newborns were buried, others around the rim where valuables had probably been hidden to keep them safe from marauders during the unattended days. The silver jewellery and ornaments he'd seen little sign of since his arrival had gone with their owners. With the whisky still buzzing in their heads, the Hmong had packed their valuables and their opium nuggets and their salted pig meat and they'd left. And Siri had slept through it all. His chest felt empty as if some important organ had been removed from it. He held the *pa n'tow* to his nose and breathed in the strength and youth of his General Bao and the courage of her tribe.

If he hadn't been so dehydrated, he might have even managed a tear or two. Something about the countryside released the emotions that remained bottled in the city. Perhaps he wasn't just sad for the plight of these friends, perhaps it was a global, all-encompassing sadness that included his whole country, and the hopelessness of life, and the fact that there would never really be peace in the world because man was intrinsically stupid. At that moment, with the mother of all hangovers pounding in his head, he felt he shouldered the misery of every victim in the universe.

He gulped down several mouthfuls of water from the communal urn and carried a bowl to the hut of weak-minded Assistant Haeng. The judge had that soggy grey look of someone who'd slept too long. Siri dribbled water into his mouth and watched him swallow in his sleep. He folded the judge's indigo hands across his chest so he looked like a gloved body in a coffin.

'Rest in peace,' he said, and left the judge to collect more dreams that might absorb and overwhelm his confusing reality of the past few days.

Siri made his way up the hill, passed the charred and still smoking remains of the haunted house, and carried on over the crest and down the hidden trail they'd walked the day before. The feeling of unrest was particularly strong here but at least he now knew what malevolent spirits he was dealing with. It was a steep drop to the valley but Siri had lived in mountains for a large chunk of his life. He negotiated the rocky trail like a goat. It wasn't long before he reached the transporter, almost completely shrouded in jungle.

'Don't worry,' Siri called. 'It's me, Yeh Ming. I'm alone.'

The boy appeared behind him on the narrow trail with a fearsome-looking submachine gun.

'Good morning, sir,' he said, like a high-school student addressing his teacher.

'How's my patient?'

'She's very fine, sir. Very fine.'

He led Siri to the back of the plane where Chamee lay on a bunched-up parachute. She was a far better colour than she'd been the day before. He checked the pulse and temperature of the little mother and asked permission to look at the incision. She nodded and talked to the roof of the plane while he checked his handiwork.

'Bao came,' she said.

'What?' He stopped.

'Bao, she came to see me early this morning.'

'Really? How on earth did she find you?'

'You told her we were here.'

'Even so, it isn't the easiest trail to pick up, especially before light.'

'Our Bao is special.'

'Yes, I think she is. And?'

He was pleased with the wound and began to change the dressing.

'She was kind. She pretended to be mad at first. But then she said she understood what we did. She knew people would be disgusted with us and it was better for the girls if they were raised by the others. But she didn't want us to disappear. She said if I had a problem I should try to contact her through our clan.'

'That was good of her.'

'Yes, she's given me hope. She gave me a message for you too.'

Siri tried to hang on to his professional demeanor. 'Oh?'

'She said you and your assistant should stay where you are and that you'll be rescued soon.'

'Oh, I see. How could she be so sure of that?'

'The *geng*.'

'Of course.'

Siri had changed the dressing and was confident there would be no problem. She was a hardy young thing and would live to be a hundred, he told her.

'And she said for me to tell you . . .' She smiled at her boy husband. 'That she's sorry she couldn't marry you yet but she has to guide her people to safety. She'll come back to you after they've found a new home.'

'What a silly thing to say,' Siri blushed.

'She loves you, Yeh Ming.'

Siri busied himself with bandages and lint.

'And, of course, I'm very fond of her. In a sort of great-grandfatherly kind of way.' He was annoyed that he'd felt it necessary to categorize his love. The young soldier contributed to the emotion of the moment without the slightest embarrassment.

'And we love you too, sir. Me and Chamee. If you weren't here my woman would be dead by now. We'll always remember you and say prayers to you at the ceremony of the ancestors.'

'Well, I'm not exactly dead yet but, of course, it was my

pleasure,' Siri said. He'd topped himself up with water in the village so his eyes watered nicely at the sight of this pretty pair in front of him. 'And perhaps I could ask you a favour.'

'Anything,' the boy said.

'The fliers. The men who were in this plane when it went down.'

'They were American pilots, sir. I buried their remains. I gave them a decent send off.'

'A Hmong funeral?'

'Just a little one, sir. As best as I could remember it.'

'That was very good of you. But their souls aren't content where they are. They want to go home.'

The boy nodded and Chamee squeezed his hand.

'I can understand that. We've felt something here.'

'I need to find their families.'

'They didn't have dog tags, sir. The American fliers at Long Chen weren't encouraged to wear them because they weren't supposed to be here.'

'Never mind, son.' Siri nodded. 'We have the number of the plane. It shouldn't be that hard to identify them. Where are they?'

Siri walked forlornly down the hill to the village with the remains of Daniel (Danny) San Souci and Eric Stone wrapped in a strip of tarpaulin. Their names were on personal letters they'd carried with them, probably against regulations. But the men who fought the secret war were tough, experienced pilots who lived every day as if it were the last because, for many of them, it was. These two had probably outweighed Siri by a few hundred pounds when they were alive, but now he carried them both under one arm. They were the reason why the Otherworld had been set in a Western city on Siri's journey. The spirits of Danny and Eric had erected the scenery. It was they, not Chamee, who had coaxed Siri to the beyond. Theirs were the souls that needed rescuing from limbo, not hers. It wasn't clear how the green button had made it into the rock pool, but it had obviously belonged to one of the pilots. When they saw it, the spirits could sense how close Siri had come to finding their remains. It had given them hope. It was his duty now to put them to rest.

The village was laid out before him, lifeless and without soul. Lumps of disused buildings perched on a hillside. Then something moved by the main house. At first he thought it might be Judge Haeng out looking for some new way to do away with himself, but as he got closer he could see a pony tethered there. A Hmong girl sat on the outside bench. He quickened his pace, but when he rounded the house he saw Dia skimming her sandalled feet over the dust.

'Dia, what's wrong?'

'Hello, Yeh Ming. Nothing big,' she said. 'I'm the fastest rider so they sent me back to let you know what we decided. I have to catch up with them.'

He sat on the bench beside her.

'What happened?'

'We met another group. They were on their way to join the big march too. They told Elder Long about relatives of theirs who'd gone before. They'd travelled at night to avoid PL patrols and the Vietnamese troops. They said a lot of the PL soldiers still hate us from the war and they kill our people on sight. No arrest, just bang bang. They had to be very quiet so they wouldn't be spotted. In the daytime the Hmong could sleep somewhere hidden away, but . . .'

She looked at the distance and tried to steady her voice.

'But what?'

'But often the group's location was given away by little children. A baby would cry and the PL would find the group and kill all of them. Some groups were so afraid they abandoned mothers and infants or they accidentally suffocated the babies trying to keep them quiet.'

'That's awful.'

'So, Elder Long thought . . .' She looked sheepish.

'Where are they?'

She smiled and pointed to the shaman's hut.

'Elder Long says it will just be until we get to Thailand. He says for you to give me an address and he'll contact you and we can find a way to get them over the river. He said you'd know a way because you're Yeh Ming.'

Siri's laughter filled the valleys around. It was apparent from the look on her face that Dia couldn't understand why this was so funny. She'd rather expected him to be angry. But Siri had his reason. The prophesy had come true in the most roundabout way. Two months earlier, Auntie Bpoo, the transvestite fortune-teller, had predicted Siri would be married and have two children before the rains started. At the time it hadn't seemed credible, not to mention physically possible. Now he had no choice but to formally add one more branch of sorcery to his list of irrational beliefs. Fortune-telling had become a science. Soon there'd be nothing but politics left to dismiss as bunkum.

'Oh, I brought you back a goat as well,' Dia said.

'Two babies and a goat on one little pony. You should be in the circus.'

'Bao said you'd need it 'cause she didn't think you'd be able to breast-feed the twins yourself.'

'Very thoughtful of her.'

'And she said she misses you.'

'Tell her I miss her too. I miss all of you. I won't sleep till I know you're safe in Thailand.'

Dia climbed onto her pony and turned three circuits until they were pointed in the right direction.

'Oh, and there's a platoon of PL soldiers two ridges across. You might want to do something to get their attention. They've got the same sense of direction as your assistant,' she laughed. 'Bye, Yeh Ming.'

Siri stood and watched her ride off. They were all so positive, so good-humoured. They were setting off on a journey of a hundred and fifty kilometres through hostile country. When they reached the limits of the lands they knew and trusted, they would abandon the animals and cover the final stretch on foot. The odds of all of them making it were poor. Yet they could still joke and talk of adventure. In their hearts they must have known that the lives their families had lived for centuries were to become legend.

Siri said good morning to the twins, selected a particularly splendid Zippo from the collection, and returned to set fire to the main hut.

15

QUIET AS THE MORGUE

The brand-new Mi-8 helicopter touched down directly on the grounds of Mahosot Hospital. Until the warranty ran out it would continue to have a Russian pilot at the controls, which explains why it didn't remove the hospital roof or land in the trees. It did, however, manage to blow all of the new chrysanthemums out of their bed. Stretcher bearers crouching low ran to the open hatchway, carefully lifted Judge Haeng onto the canvas, and whisked him away. The helicopter could have taken him to the temporary field hospital in Sam Neua in the north, but Siri had insisted the man's condition was so grave they had no choice but to take him directly to Vientiane.

It mattered not a jot to Siri that the judge had no condition to speak of. Apart from the broken wrist, once his boss had slept off the drug, he would be his old disagreeable self within twenty-four hours. Siri was just tired and he wanted to go home. Despite the incomprehensible ranting of the pilot, he insisted on remaining on board until the rotors had stopped spinning. He decided he was already short enough, thank you, and he preferred a dignified homecoming.

French medical and US military choppers had arrived frequently at the hospital during the war years but, four years later, all flights had stopped. So it wasn't surprising that doctors and nurses and patients came spilling out of their buildings to look at the spectacularly gleaming Russian craft. To Siri's profound disappointment, Dtui and Geung were not among them. He'd hoped to impress them.

He handed the twins, now crying in coordinated stereo, to two maternity nurses and asked them to take care of the infants. He told them he'd stop by later. He walked to the morgue, carrying the remains of Danny and Eric under his arm, his only luggage. One of the uprooted chrysanthemums lay on the morgue's welcome mat as if it were insisting on an autopsy. The door was padlocked and for some mysterious reason his key didn't work. He wondered why they'd needed to change a three-month-old lock. He went to the office window but the curtains were drawn tightly and there was no gap to allow him to see inside.

It was just after five and usually Dtui and Geung would be heading off to water the squashes in the cooperative plot behind the hospital. They understandably dawdled getting there so it wasn't unheard of for the morgue to remain open till five thirty. They certainly wouldn't have rushed away before five. He had to consider another obvious possibility. On his last protracted interstate trip, the hospital had drafted Siri's staff to work in other departments. He thought he'd kicked up enough of a stink about it to ensure it wouldn't happen again but he wouldn't put anything past the current administration.

He stopped by Urology and wandered in to the office of Dr Mut. 'Wandering in' was a standard procedure in most Vientiane offices. Doors were usually left ajar due to the heat and a lot of the buildings were open plan. Apart from personages of the absolute top of the heap, there were no receptionists or secretaries to keep out unwanted guests. So riff-raff was to be expected.

'Good health, Mut,' Siri said.

The doctor was staring at two plastic cups that sat in front of him on the desk. He looked up and smiled. He was a kindly, greasy-faced man with hair slicked to his scalp like trails of paint.

'Ah, Siri. Can I tempt you?'

'Can't say I'm sure what you're asking me to do,' Siri confessed, not knowing whether these were specimens or oolong tea.

'I always end the day with a hot ginseng. Keeps me active in the bedroom.' He winked, threw back one of the cups, and wiped his lips.

'I'll pass, thank you, Mut. Being active all by yourself makes you blind.'

Mut laughed. 'Word on the ward is that you'll be rabbiting soon on a regular basis. Young bride. Disgusting. Envy you, though.'

He threw back the other cup.

'Shouldn't you be savouring that?'

'No. Horrible stuff. Don't want it to last a minute longer than necessary. Tastes like pubic-hair roots. Gets stuck between your teeth the same too. Know what I mean?'

Siri had always found it fitting that the head of Urology should be so adept at toilet humour. Mut was its grand master.

'Well, seeing as you know so much about everything,' Siri said, 'and seeing as you stole my nurse last time I turned my back, I thought perhaps you'd know what's become of my morgue people.'

'Ooh!'

Mut let the end of the 'ooh' trail into a long noisy breath. 'Now that I can't tell you, comrade.'

'Because you don't know or because it's a secret?'

'Mystery, Siri. Mystery. Nobody has any idea. That morgue's been locked like that for several days now. Nobody seems to have a sound idea why. But there are rumours, Siri. Lots of 'em.'

'I'm listening.'

'Something happened, they say. Your Nurse Dtui and her policeman got caught up in something nasty.'

'And?'

'That's all I heard.'

'That's not much help.'

'Sorry, comrade. All I know.'

Siri, anxiety growing with every stride, hurried to the administration building. As it was after five, he wasn't surprised to find it devoid of administrators. None of the clerical staff there knew anything beyond the same rumour passed on by Mut. His frustration grew. He knew how unconcerned Dtui and Phosy were for their own safety. It was like them to get into trouble. He went to Mr Geung's dormitory room but his neighbour admitted he hadn't seen Geung for three or four days. The mystery was thickening.

Siri's Triumph was in the parking lot where he'd left it before he headed north. He wiped a thick brown layer of dust from it and tried the key. It charged into life first time. He had to hand it to the British. If nothing else, they knew how to make motorcycles. He attached Danny and Eric to the back of the seat and headed to Madame Daeng's shop. The shutter was bolted and a sign, not in Daeng's own hand, was taped to the front of it. It read,

SORRY, CUSTOMERS. CLOSED TILL FURTHER NOTICE.

He wasn't sure where to turn next. He knew it was a mistake but he stopped by his house out beyond the That Luang Stupa. The place was a menagerie of his own making. Through his benevolence it had become a guest-house for strays, some of whom he hadn't yet met. Mrs Fah's kids were running around like headless chicks, shaking off the cobwebs they'd gathered at school. Inthanet, the puppeteer, was having a serious fight with his girlfriend, Miss Vong, in the kitchen. Something about a wife he'd forgotten to mention. Comrade Noo, the forest monk who was in hiding from the Thai junta of the month, was giving a seminar to half a dozen students in the back-yard. And two attractive young ladies he didn't know sat in his room watching a TV he didn't own.

None of the inhabitants could shed light on the events at the morgue and he realized staying at the house would do him no good. He grabbed some fresh clothes from one of the two piles the women were leaning against and retired to the bathroom. He tried to ignore the brassieres in lurid colours that hung there, had a quick shower, and fled. At the door, he ran into Mrs Fah coming back from the market with instant noodles for her brood.

'Dr Siri. When did you get back?' she asked. Siri was delighted at least one person had noticed his absence. 'We heard you'd been kidnapped.'

She didn't seem all that concerned. It was as if 'kidnapped' and 'bitten by a mosquito' might have carried the same weight in her addled mind.

'I escaped.'

'That's nice.'

'Mrs Fah, have you heard anything from Dtui or Phosy?'

'No, Doctor. Since she moved out, I haven't heard a thing.'

'Has there been any news around?'

He didn't mean newspaper news or radio news. He wasn't particularly interested in crop yield or cooperative farming advances. He meant reliable social hearsay news such as was in ready supply at the markets.

'Nothing much. They say there was a killing out at Kok Pho. Plenty of police out there. Just rumours, probably. Like some noodles, Doctor?'

But when she looked back he was already on his bike.

What in the blazes was happening? He needed answers and there was only one person he could rely on to provide them. He sped out along the Phonkeing Road. The potholes were more challenging than he remembered and there were several occasions when his hands were the only parts of him in contact with the bike. He skidded left at kilometre 6, sped along the side road, and soon found himself surrounded by boys with big guns at the entrance to the government compound. In spite of the fact that he'd been there a thousand times they still insisted on escorting him to Civilai's house. His friend might be retired now but he still had his security rating.

From the kerbside in front of the little bungalow, Siri sat on his saddle and yelled. 'Old brother, could you come out here and tell this midget I'm not a threat to national security?'

It was dark now and the light on the porch went on and the door opened. But it was Civilai's wife, Madame Nong, who stood there smiling.

'Well, if it isn't the second most handsome man in Laos,' she said in her songlike Luang Prabang lilt.

'You know this man?' the little guard asked. It seemed to Siri that if the government didn't insist on changing sentries every week they might save themselves a lot of effort.

'It's fine,' she said. 'He's harmless.'

The escort rode away and Siri climbed off his bike. He went through the silly little American gate that any horse or bullock could have stepped over and kissed Nong's cheek. She too was a product of a French education so she didn't recoil from physical contact like the wives of her Vietnamese-trained neighbours.

'I was hoping to see the old man,' Siri said.

'I was hoping too. He's been gone all this week.'

'Gone where?'

'Don't know.'

'Come on. There's nothing you two don't share.'

'I'm serious. He came home one day in a fit of nervous excitement, packed a few clothes, told me not to worry, and left.'

'He's retired.'

'It doesn't feel like it. He'd been working on something with your Nurse Dtui and Inspector Phosy.'

'Did he say what?'

'Look, dust yourself off and come inside. I'll make you a little drinkie and tell you all I know.'

'My fantasy.'

'What?'

'Civilai out of town . . .'

'Dream on, Casanova. I still keep my Luger under the pillow.'

'That's encouraging. At least we make it to the bedroom.'

*

At the kitchen table, Nong told Siri everything she knew – about the booby trap, the poisoned cakes – everything up to the day Phosy and Dtui decided to follow up on a lead they had about the Lizard studying at Dong Dok. Civilai had come home that day, flustered and secretive, grabbed a bag of clothes, told her not to worry, and was gone in twenty minutes.

'And, of course, you've worried,' Siri assumed.

'It's been three days. Of course, he used to do things like this all the time when he was in the politburo. I wouldn't see him for weeks at a time. But he's not supposed to be doing anything official these days. That means he's doing things he shouldn't. Ornery old men can get themselves in a lot of trouble, Siri.'

'Well, if he was dead you would have heard by now.'

'That's very comforting, thank you.'

'Have you asked around?'

'All his old comrades. Nobody seems to know anything. It's as if my darling husband has just vanished off the face of the earth.'

'Don't panic, my love. I'll find him.'

Every step, every line of inquiry had made the mystery even more baffling. He had one more stop to make before he would allow hopelessness to overtake him. Phosy had an office at police headquarters at the Interior Department. It was one of the few buildings where the wandering-in policy didn't apply. A scruffy man in a large green uniform sat at the desk. His hair was so short it was more pink than black. He seemed surprised to have a visitor after dark.

'Help you?'

'I'm looking for Inspector Phosy.'

'No.'

'No what?'

'Haven't seen him all week.'

'Do you have any idea . . . ?'

'No. I just man the desk. If you have any inquiries—'

'I know. Ask in the morning when someone with a mind is on duty.'

'Hey, no need to be rude, old man.'

Siri took a deep breath and reminded himself where he was.

'Look, I'm sorry. This isn't police business. I'm a friend of the inspector. I haven't seen him for a few days and I'm worried about him.' Just for effect he added, 'I'm Siri Paiboun, the national coroner.'

'Then I reckon I've heard of you.'

'Could you just give me a hint?'

The night man looked up into Siri's tired eyes and obviously decided he wasn't a threat to security.

'All I can tell you is that something big went down earlier in the week and your pal was caught up in it. Him and a couple of other people have been missing since. Nobody's saying what happened to them. We've had the director of police and half a dozen Vietnamese advisers here running around. But I didn't tell you this.'

Siri's was the only engine disturbing the silence in Vientiane that night. He'd reached the stage where he didn't know what to do, who to ask. The fatigue of the past few days was squeezing rational thought out of him. With no idea how much precious petrol there was in his tank, he rode around the streets of Vientiane's humble downtown. It was a grid of no more than twenty blocks, most of them dark, deserted, and uninviting. Few Lao could afford a night out and for those who could, the curfew had them home by ten. The resident foreigners had their favourite spots and kept them alive. Ninety per cent of the entertainment venues had closed down since the Royalists left and the remainder were pale shadows of their lively pasts.

Siri had no idea why he was still there. If he'd been looking for inspiration, it didn't come. He'd ridden four times past Daeng's shop and banged on the shutters twice. He'd stopped at the spot on the bank of the Mekhong where he and Civilai ate their baguette lunches and solved the problems of the universe together. His heart felt heavy in his old chest. He didn't want to assume the worst but the worst kept tapping him on the shoulder.

Finally, he stopped at a *roti* stall down by the old deserted Odeon cinema. He figured sugar might be the solution. He ate two sweet condensed-milk *roti* with castor sugar sprinkles and ordered a third before it occurred to him he hadn't eaten since the pork the previous evening. What a different place, time, and dimension that all seemed now.

'Siri?'

The voice from behind him was warm. He turned to see Bassak, one of the clerks from the Department of Justice. He was waiting for a girl to fill an order at the minced-fowl stand beside Siri's.

'Good health, Bassak.'

'It's good to see you alive, Siri. Welcome back.'

'Thank you.'

'I hear the judge made it back too.'

Siri shrugged.

'Never mind,' Bassak sighed. 'So you'd all be out celebrating then?'

'No, just can't sleep. You know how it is? It's like travelling by air. Once you land, your soul takes a while to forget it's flying.'

'Never flown myself.'

Bassak collected his spicy minced duck and climbed onto his bicycle.

'What did you mean, "you all"?' Siri asked.

'What's that, comrade?'

'You said, "You'd all be out celebrating."'

'Oh, I assumed you'd just left the others.'

'What others?'

'I just dropped off some quails' eggs at the Russian Club. The wife raises quail for a bit of extra cash. They're a bit like chickens: eat whatever you feel like giving them. We can make about . . .'

'Comrade, who did you see?'

'Your people, Dtui and Geung. I can't see them turning up for work on time tomorrow.'

'What? Why?'

'I don't know who's footing the bill but there seemed to be enough beer bottles on the table to put the glass factory on double shift again.'

'You're sure it was them?'

'Come on, Siri. How likely is it I'd mistake Geung and Dtui for any other couple?'

16

THE RUSSIAN CLUB

The Russian Club wasn't a club and it wasn't exclusively for Russians. It was a wooden restaurant, open to the elements on three sides, that sat brazenly beside the Mekhong. Two of its music speakers were deliberately turned towards the river to disturb the Thais. There was probably a pair of binoculars or two trained on the clientele most nights, perhaps even a camera with a telescopic lens. The customers of the Russian Club liked to boast of their inclusion in Thai anti-communist files whenever they enjoyed a night out there.

The club had once been a favourite haunt of foreign correspondents, the last of whom had been kicked out earlier that year. Now the only news to escape the country was gleaned from the gossip of refugees. The place had been taken over by Eastern European experts, Vietnamese advisers, the odd expatriate diplomat, and one or two foreign teachers who had, curiously, been allowed to stay. Lao were in the minority and included guests and counterparts of the experts, those with connections, and those who had converted their savings to gold before the value of the *kip* plummeted to below that of used cigarette papers.

Not wanting to leave Danny and Eric unguarded on the back of the motorcycle, Siri carried them up the steps and into the busy restaurant. He walked along the rows of tables and the patrons there, assuming he was selling something, either averted their eyes or waved him away.

The table he was searching for stood back near the serving hatch. Had there been a national lottery, this certainly would have been the scene of the grand prize winning victory party. Defeated plates were piled high at its centre and empty bottles were crammed onto the white tablecloth like penguins on a rapidly melting iceberg. Around it sat characters with faces as red and expressive as the villains in Chinese operas.

Civilai and Madame Daeng conspired on the far side. Mr Geung, famous for becoming intoxicated on half a glass of straw-fruit juice, was glowing like a New Year's lantern. Phosy was laughing at the joke of some gentleman in uniform. Only one person sat sober, relishing the atmosphere and popping spring rolls into her mouth. It was Dtui who first caught sight of the doctor.

'Dr Siri!' she announced to the whole restaurant and, presumably, to the Thai military opposite. The cheer from his colleagues prompted the Europeans to raise their own glasses and toast the newcomer. His friends gathered around him and patted his back and dragged another chair across for him to join them. He was placed between Daeng and Mr Geung. Daeng took hold of his hand.

'Did somebody's birthday slip my memory?' Siri asked. His relief at finding them alive filled him with joy.

'We've been to court,' shouted Civilai. He put his arm around the soldier. 'This learned gentleman is our barrister.'

The table cheered again, raised their glasses to the barrister, and ordered more beer. The soldier saluted, inadvertently poking himself in the eye as he did so. The party had evidently been going on for some while.

'Well, the verdict was obviously in your favour,' Siri decided.

'It was never in doubt if the truth be told,' Phosy slurred.

A fresh plate arrived and Siri was plied with a little of everything that was left over.

'I trust you're going to tell me all about it,' Siri said, opting for beer with ice cubes, a rare luxury.

'All in good time,' said Civilai. 'First a toast to our returned hero. To Siri, for completing a perfect day.'

All of them filled, then raised, then emptied their glasses.

'Good to see you back, Doc,' Dtui said, raising her green Fanta bottle. She refilled Siri's beer glass with the other hand.

'And now,' Phosy announced, 'Dr Siri will tell us all about his abduction.'

'I'd rather . . .' Siri began but was drowned out by another cheer and the clinking of cutlery on empty bottles.

And so, for half an hour, Siri recounted the highlights of his adventures in the north-east leaving out his shamanic journey to the Otherworld and not mentioning General Bao at all. The audience managed to be spellbound and raucous at the same time. He had them crying with mirth as he described Judge Haeng's exploits and he saw tears in Dtui's eyes when he told them of the plight of the Hmong. Daeng held on to him the whole time and stared into his gorgeous green eyes.

Once he was drained of stories, he insisted they tell him why they were celebrating. But the curfew beat them to it. The taped music stopped midsong and already policemen on bicycles sat by the roadside, more of a reminder than a threat. Drinking large amounts of alcohol night after night begins to form a chemical chain that eventually turns into one long state of fuddlement. All Siri had needed to do was top up his alcohol reserve. He was as drunk as any of them when they stood to leave on uneasy legs. Madame Daeng's shop was a mere two riverside blocks away so they all agreed to make their way there. Siri wisely left the motorcycle in front of the restaurant, but as he walked away he heard . . .

'Uncle! Uncle!' Their middle-aged waitress came clopping down the steps after him on clog-like sandals. In her arms she had a parcel. 'You forgot this.'

What nightmares Siri could have looked forward to if he'd left the remains of Danny and Eric under a seat in a beer hall. He'd never want to go to bed again. He thanked the waitress with a tip and refused to tell her what exactly the parcel contained.

At Madame Daeng's the general feeling was that they'd all had more than enough to drink so why not have some more. She opened two bottles of rice whisky and set about boiling water for coffee. The food was settling in the stomachs of the revellers so the mood was slightly less playful although there wasn't a moment when someone or other wasn't raising a laugh. The barrister, it turned out, wasn't a barrister at all. He was a driver, which Civilai pointed out was far more useful than a barrister. He was attached to the Security Division and he had to return their truck in one piece. So he opted for coffee as did Dtui and Mr Geung.

'Right,' Siri shouted at last. 'Is anybody going to tell me where the funding came from for the overindulgence tonight? I know you didn't dip into the morgue budget 'cause that wouldn't have covered the first plate of river shrimp.'

'It was a sort of . . . donation,' Phosy said.

'Our benefactor told us to go and have a good time,' Dtui added. 'So we did.'

'And who was that?'

'The woman who tried to kill you when you weren't here,' Dtui told him, bringing a sobering coffee to everyone at the table.

'I . . . I did . . . n't kill the auditors,' Geung stated proudly.

'You certainly didn't,' Dtui told him. She patted his hand. At last his conscience was clear.

'Why on earth not?' Siri asked. 'I would have.'

'We know you would,' she laughed. 'That's why they sneaked in while you were away.'

'You know' – Siri was getting frustrated – 'why don't we just start at the beginning and tell old Uncle Siri exactly what he's missed.'

And so they did. Like puzzlers putting together an enormous jigsaw, they provided Siri with the pieces of their story. Siri's head flicked back and forth as they each contributed their parts, adding missing details and colour, and, in Civilai's case, the odd fabrication. At one stage the driver excused himself and left. But the story continued to the point where Phosy and Dtui were in the kitchen surrounded by geriatric villains with guns. Siri, a mystery devotee, was captivated.

'So, don't stop,' he pleaded. 'What happened?'

'Ah, well,' Civilai said. 'For the sake of prolonging the tension, we've omitted one or two small details. With your permission, ladies and gentlemen, I shall fill in the gaps.'

He stood for effect.

'You see? At our meeting the previous evening, the one where Mrs Bounlan so conveniently showed up . . .'

'Dropped onto our plate like the answer to a prayer, you might say,' Phosy added.

'Thank you. At that meeting, we had agreed to treat anything out of the ordinary as a potential threat. We knew how clever the Lizard could be and we had to be just as devious.'

'If we hadn't come to that decision when we did,' Madame Daeng called from the hearth, 'we might have gone along with Bounlan's story.'

'She was most convincing,' Civilai agreed. 'While she was still there we even made the mistake of deciding that Phosy and Dtui would go out to Dong Dok the next day. I'm sure she was delighted. They'd expected us to follow that lead blindly. The Royalists destroyed all the student records before they fled so it was unlikely we could be sure who had been enrolled in which courses. But they didn't destroy the financial files. The Department of Education has records of all the courses they offered in the year Bounlan mentioned. I paid the records office a visit first thing the next morning and the clerk was only too pleased to go through the files with me. They were somewhat mildewy and rat gnawed but still in order.'

'There was no in-service course for external teachers in 1964,' Phosy interrupted.

'If I may continue,' Civilai huffed, 'there was no course for external teachers in 1965, 1966 or '67 or '68. In fact, Dong Dok didn't run any external courses at all in those days. Red light number one.'

'Meanwhile,' Dtui joined in, 'Phosy and I were having a leisurely breakfast at home. Civilai got a note to us telling us Bounlan had been lying and our Plan 34B should go into effect.'

'Actually, there was just the one plan,' Daeng put in. 'We assumed someone would be watching Dtui and Phosy so we made it obvious they'd be going to Dong Dok without an armed escort.'

'I called the hospital on the communal police dormitory phone and told them I'd be at the college,' Dtui said. 'And Phosy worked on the Vespa.'

'Civilai collected me on his motorcycle,' Daeng said. 'The car would have been too conspicuous. We took some old work clothes and guns and a few disguises I had left over from the old days and we sniffed around at Dong Dok.'

'Cleverly disguised as road sweepers,' Civilai added. 'We saw this chap hanging around the English Department. He was well dressed but he didn't seem to be going anywhere. I asked some students and they said they'd never seen him before. I watched him for a bit and what do you know? He had a walkie-talkie in his briefcase. Of course nobody at the institute is likely to question a man with a radio. They'd just assume he was a spy and leave him alone. It would appear he got a message from his lookout telling him Phosy and Dtui were on their way.'

'And he happened to just be leaving his "class" when we arrived,' Phosy said.

'There was a real Ajan Ming at the department . . .' Civilai began.

'But this wasn't him,' said Daeng.

'You can imagine them sitting around plotting it all, can't you?' Dtui said. She put on her evil-old-lady voice. '"How clever can we be to fool these communists? Let's add a little bit of irony here, a touch of religious symbolism there."'

'But you do have to remember, they had to make sure we wouldn't be alerted, wouldn't be tempted to bring in the troops,' Phosy added. 'This way they could check at each stage that it was just you and me. Very clever.'

'You sound like you admire them,' Dtui said.

'Well, no. I feel like they're sad old Royalists with too much time on their hands. But brilliant old Royalists. They wanted to make it as complicated as possible. Like Madame Daeng said, they could just as easily have lobbed in a hand grenade that night of the first meeting.'

'But then they would have had to deal with the guards,' Civilai reminded him. 'This way they could lure you away. They probably had something just as convoluted planned for me and Siri. But we digress . . . there we were at the coffee shop at Dong Dok. And when Ajan Ming suggested the cemetery . . .'

'. . . we passed that information on to our own spies,' said Phosy.

'I left a note on the coffee-shop table for our sweepers to pick up,' Dtui smiled. 'And we made it clear in front of Ming that we'd be stopping off somewhere for lunch on our way there.'

'To give our team time to arrive,' Phosy added and sipped at his coffee.

'I've never known you to stay quiet for so long,' Civilai said to Siri.

'I'm fascinated.'

'And it gets better, little brother. Daeng and I sped off to the cemetery. I adopted my "hairy mourner" disguise . . .'

'That was my wig,' Daeng added.

'. . . and I visited my dear wife's grave. I hope their God will forgive me for ripping off flowers from someone else's headstone. Shortly after I got there, a little fellow with a rake showed up. When Phosy and Dtui arrived, he started work.'

'He would have known we didn't have any way to contact the authorities. I'm sure we were followed the whole time,' Phosy said. 'So he was confident enough to send us on to the next leg of our guided ambush.'

'Our little tiff at the cemetery convinced him we'd get iced tea and then go on to the house from there.' Dtui squeezed Phosy's arm. 'I personally think we could make it on Thai daytime television.'

Mr Geung snorted a laugh. 'Ha, C . . . Comrade Dtui on Thai TV. Yes, I . . . I want to see it.'

Everyone laughed except Siri.

'Next! Next! What happened then?'

'Phosy and Dtui were tailed again,' Civilai told him. 'This time we saw him. The so-called Ajan Ming, in a baseball cap and dark glasses. He followed them all the way to the house and went in after them. The trap was sprung.'

'We'd been in public places up until then where we were sure they wouldn't try anything,' Phosy said.

'Even so, you were taking an unnecessary risk,' Siri reminded him.

'We'd been at risk every moment since the bomb was planted. This way we could at least have some say in our destiny.'

'Point taken.'

'And we believed they'd want to talk to us before they did anything. We'd foiled not one but two of their clever little assassination attempts. They wanted us to know who was in charge. They had to introduce themselves or the whole charade thing would have been for nothing. They'd want us to know there wasn't a chance of their being caught. Once we went missing, they knew the police trail would go cold after Dong Dok. They could even keep using the house. They might even have tried the cemetery routine on Comrade Civilai and Daeng. We thought they'd boast about that.'

Civilai, frustrated by all the interruptions to his narration, threw out his arms dramatically for the final scene.

'So – Phosy and Dtui are in the house of the enemy with barely a minute to live. Daeng and I had been given time to contact Phosy's squad using the password he'd told them to expect. We gave them the address and arranged to meet them there. Our mission was to keep our adversaries occupied till they arrived.'

'Armed to the teeth,' Madame Daeng joined in, 'Civilai and I enter the house, him from the rear, me from the front. Our allies are surrounded by armed killers. "Drop your weapons," we shout, as one would.'

'But they didn't,' said Civilai.

'And there they are pointing their guns at Phosy and Dtui—'

'And us pointing our guns at the villains.'

'And the Lizard woman laughs and says, "If you carry a gun, you have to be prepared to use it. And I happen to know you aren't."'

'That's when Daeng shot her,' Civilai said triumphantly.

'What?' Siri turned to his betrothed.

Daeng blushed. 'Only in the leg.'

'And I was so impressed I shot one too.' Civilai smiled. 'I got him in the thigh, I believe. The others dropped their weapons. Then this little squad of policemen charged in and Phosy ordered them about and it was all over.'

Mr Geung clapped his hands.

'We got in touch with the Security Division,' Phosy said, 'and told them who we'd caught and they sent the whole damned army over. They'd learned from earlier mistakes so they bundled the Lizard and her cronies off up to the old military stockade at Phonhong.'

'So where have you been since?' Siri asked.

'It appears we've become a revolutionary government in the eyes of the world, rather than a rebel insurgency,' Civilai said. 'We have to observe a certain protocol. The Vietnamese advisers told us we should try the gang of four as traitors rather than just shoot them. They said we would gain more leverage if their crimes were brought out in a military court. It would certainly discourage other plotters.'

'So that's where we've been,' Dtui said. 'Three solid days of giving evidence, all on the record. They went by the morgue and picked up Geung.'

'I . . . I . . . I told them about the cashew cakes . . . m . . . making me fart,' Geung boasted.

'There were no end of witnesses shipped in from all over. They connected the Lizard to this and that act of terrorism,' Civilai said. 'They filmed the whole thing. They wouldn't let us go till the tribunal was over, and we were in the middle of nowhere so we couldn't contact anyone.'

'Which reminds me,' Siri interrupted. 'Speaking of wives and forgiveness . . .'

'Fear not, Siri,' said Civilai. 'I sent a message to Madame Nong as soon as they released us from security this afternoon. She's probably packing for her next Women's Union excursion as we speak.'

'So you stayed for the verdict?'

'The four of them had kept silent,' Phosy said. 'They knew there was no point in putting up a defence. They were found guilty of treason.'

'And the punishment?'

'A firing squad in the morning,' Daeng told him. 'They asked if we'd like to stay and watch but we were keen to get home to our loved ones. The driver had us back here by seven. We went directly to the Russian Club. We'd been at the stockade for three days. We needed to unwind and eat some decent food.'

'And the bill?'

'I was leaving the courtroom,' Dtui said. 'Actually, it was a tent, and the Lizard asked permission to give me something. She told me how impressed she was with us. She said perhaps her country wasn't in such bad hands after all with people like us around. And she gave me her ring off her finger. She said it wasn't that valuable but it should be worth enough to get us a good night out on her. She said the manageress at the Russian Club had taken jewellery from her before when she didn't have any cash, no questions asked. She was right. The whole bill was covered.'

'So the ring was probably worth four times that,' said cynical old Civilai.

They all sipped at their coffee now and drank water to sober up. One of the whisky bottles hadn't been touched at all. A mellow, satisfied feeling melted over them like honey. Two jobs well done.

'And there I was thinking I'd had an interesting few days,' Siri said.

17

INDIGNATIONHOOD

Hmong New Year passed virtually unnoticed in Vientiane and, as December held no other significant dates for celebration, January arrived unannounced. The weather, for once, gave nobody cause for complaint. The sky was blue and cloudless and the city was fanned day and night by cooling breezes. Locals had taken to wearing mufflers round their necks and socks inside their flip-flops. Walkers everywhere crunched through unswept leaves. The pool at the Lan Xang Hotel was off-limits because the water was cold and the lifeguard refused to jump in if anyone got into trouble. Although the Lao wouldn't have their own new year for another three months, the West was calling this 1978 and hailing it as the dawning of the age of computers. Half a million were already in use around the world and predictions were that this number might double by the end of the century. Like the news of Charlie Chaplin's death and the decision by Sweden to ban aerosol cans, the revelation passed Vientiane by without even staring in the window.

For reasons best known to himself, Judge Haeng had taken to using a cane following the trauma of his ordeal in the north-east. There was nothing at all wrong with his leg but Siri assumed that once the cast was off his arm he had no cause to tell strangers of his bravery otherwise.

'There must have been thirty of them,' he'd declare, gazing out into the misty beyond of his memory. 'Tough, mountain warriors, trained to kill. They picked off Siri straight away but I was able to evade them for four days, living wild in the jungle. Surviving off the land. Hampered by life-threatening injuries, I relied on training from my days in the underground to get through it all. A good socialist must be ambidextrous: able to chop down a mighty teak tree with his left hand and darn a shirt with his right. You have to understand the jungle to love and respect it like a wife.

'After a while I felt concerned about Dr Siri. He isn't a young man and we must have compassion for our senior citizens. I went in search of him. I feared not for my own life but ultimately I succumbed to my injuries and to the dreaded malaria. See this bruising on my hands? Further evidence of the ravages of the disease.'

Siri had smiled when the story made it back to him. Only Haeng could have caught malaria at that altitude. It wasn't till the Hmong were forced down to lower elevations that the mosquito joined the list of their enemies. Siri waited for the day when he'd be summoned to the Department of Justice to find Haeng with a nose so long he couldn't get out of his office. Siri, meanwhile, had one or two cases a week to keep himself and his team moderately busy.

Nothing more was heard of the Lizard and her cohorts but a nasty thought had crossed Siri's mind. These were the days when people could vanish without a physical trace and, over time, be deleted completely from memory. But one matter still lingered and made the old doctor shake his head from time to time. Why, he wondered, would a woman about to be executed make a gift of a valuable ring to the very people who had condemned her to death? Was it merely a final act of bravado from an arrogant woman or had there been one spell left in her cauldron? According to the Security Division, the firing squad had done its duty on the morn, but would they admit to losing the Lizard a second time? The manageress still presided over her clients at the Russian Club and nothing untoward had happened to suggest anything had gone wrong. Siri had nothing but a creeping tingle at the back of his neck to keep him company.

Fortunately, he had something else to occupy his mind. Following his return from Xiang Khouang, Siri had taken up a cause. He had canvassed both the Lao and Vietnamese military in an effort to make them accountable for their handling of Hmong refugees. He wanted a commitment that they would have safe passage when fleeing to Thailand. It was Civilai's opinion that if Siri hadn't been friendly with certain influential members of the military he too would have vanished without a trace for such foolishness. Siri countered that he was just reminding them of their own policy.

'According to your politburo, the Hmong are Lao citizens,' he told Civilai. 'The official line is, "All Lao citizens are equal before the law irrespective of ethnic origin." They have the same rights as we do.'

'And we have rights?'

'By comparison.'

'Keep on pushing the army, you stubborn old fart, and we'll see how strong your rights are.'

So Siri, being Siri, kept on pushing. He ran into the same rehashed diatribe about national security and the US-led insurgency but not one sensible argument as to why unarmed women and children and old people posed a threat to the nation. If they were dangerous then surely the army ought to be glad they were leaving. It soon became clear that the issue was not a centrally agreed upon policy but rather left up to the whim of the regional army commander in each of the provinces. He heard that some units coming across caravans of Hmong escorted them back home and sent the seniors for re-education, where they learned that this was a multicultural society and even the most impoverished and ignorant had an opportunity for advancement. But the officers he spoke to also conceded there might be the odd patrol leader with a well-founded grudge who would execute first and consider the moral implications later over a drink.

He heard more disturbing rumours that the new Soviet planes were being used to drop liquid chemicals on caravans of refugees although that wasn't a policy anyone he spoke to cared to discuss. Whatever the truth, an alarming number of refugees fleeing their homes weren't reaching the camps in Thailand and Siri didn't like that fact. But, as Civilai said, he was getting closer to that "Has anyone seen Siri lately?" moment. For a month he had attempted to beg a brief interview with Commander Khoumki, the chief of staff of the armed forces. He'd known the lad in the field and had once removed a bullet from his intestines. Under fire in the jungle he'd considered their relationship to be a close one. But Khoumki had risen through the ranks and left all those non-profit forest love affairs behind. Now he was inaccessible and would have remained so had Siri not crossed the line.

It was obvious that playing by the rules wasn't getting him anywhere so he resorted to the unthinkable. He spent one afternoon in the cutting room painting a large sign. It read,

WE NEED ANSWERS ON THE PLIGHT
OF OUR HMONG BROTHERS

There hadn't been a protest since the PL dragged students onto the street to rally spontaneously against the fascist dictatorial military clique in Thailand. That had been a year earlier. Nobody was foolish enough to hassle a paranoid government at a time when civil rights was a luxury of the decadent West. But the lone Siri took one afternoon off work and carried his placard down to the front of the Khaosan Pathet Lao News Agency office. On his way he stopped at various government departments, the police station, and Madame Daeng's shop to announce his intention. He was at the gate of the news agency no more than five minutes before a truckload of soldiers arrived and wrestled him onto the back of the truck.

This was a dilemma for the authorities. Siri was a forty-something-year member of the Party and a borderline national hero. Everyone in the politburo knew him. He had friends in the military who respected him. Plus, as there were no laws, he couldn't technically have broken one. They weren't able to quietly spirit him away as he'd been very loud in stating his intentions. He'd gathered a nice crowd and there were photographs of the arrest. They could have arranged a small 'accident', of course, but instead they called him into the office and asked him what exactly he wanted.

An invitation was delivered to him the day after his release by a surprisingly tall guard in an unprecedentedly ironed uniform. It read:

Commander Khoumki requests the company of Dr Siri Paiboun at his private residence for a soirée on January 14. Formal evening attire. 6 PM.
RSVP.

Siri rolled his eyes when he showed it to Dtui.

'So now the head of the socialist armed forces is having a soirée? A man who ran operations from a cave in Huaphan is telling people how to dress? There must have been a chapter in the manual I missed: "How to Fill the Velvet Slippers of the Royalists without Anyone's Noticing." The arrogance of it.'

'So you aren't going?'

'If there's no other way for a knave to greet a king I suppose I have no choice. Dust off my purple tuxedo, miss. I shall go to the ball.'

The commander's house was so new the smell of paint overpowered the incense. It looked at first glance like an early attempt at man-powered flight that had crashed and crumpled. It was obviously something Khoumki had seen in a magazine and ordered built. It stood in the centre of an acre of land surrounded by an eight-foot wall topped with broken bottles set in cement. All around it were rice fields, and the damp from the paddy had already started to turn the base of the whitewashed walls yellow.

One of the six armed guards at the gate checked Siri's invitation and ID card and searched his motorcycle for concealed insurgents. Eyeing his sandals and collarless shirt with distaste, they let him pass. He parked at the end of a row of shiny black limousines and made his way to the marble steps. Another guard in full dress uniform saluted him reluctantly and seemed to smirk as Siri passed through the large double doors. A servant briskly shepherded him through the house, giving him mere seconds to savour the framed pictures and the brass candle holders and the grand piano tucked away in rooms on either side of him. Before he knew it he was outside the back door feeling like a morsel of food that had been swallowed and evacuated in one movement.

He stood on the porch and took in the scene. It was an ostentatious soirée on a vast lawn. The grass was so new the squares of turf sat like grids on a game board. The players, either in uniform or national dress or shirt and tie were positioned mid-tournament, all tactically vying for a crack at the commander. They held glasses with shrouds of tissue. Siri wondered whether that might have something to do with not wanting to leave fingerprints. The great man himself stood in an overly decorated dress uniform with his chest pushed pigeonlike toward the house. He had a throng about him.

As soon as Siri stepped down onto the spongy lawn, a soldier with a tray accosted him and forced a whisky soda on him. He sipped it. It was more of a soda whisky or rather a soda that had passed within a whisker of an open whisky bottle. He put it back on the tray and felt sufficiently insulted by it to break all the game rules. He ignored the copses of guests and went diagonally across the board in a beeline to the commander. The host was in the process of being checkmated by a woman who looked like a well-endowed gift. She was wrapped so tightly in her expensive *phasin* and *sabai* sash that all her blood had been squeezed to her face.

'Commander Khoumki,' Siri said, stepping up to him with his hand extended. The woman stood back in horror. The head of the armed forces certainly deserved a polite *nop* in greeting, hands together, head bowed low, not this. She looked around as if hoping some bouncer might come to remove this shoddy old man. The commander in turn stood with one hand on his drink and the other firmly by his side. But Siri was unmoved. He would have stood there all evening with his hand extended until he got it shaken. Khoumki could obviously envisage this so he casually obliged.

'Dr Santi,' he said, freeing his hand as quickly as possible. 'Long time no see.'

'Siri!'

'Yes? How have you been?' Khoumki turned to his guests. 'I haven't seen the doctor since the campaign of '66 in Xien Khaw. I hear he's a coroner now. Ah, there's the treasurer at last.' He excused himself from his group. 'You'll have to excuse me. Nice to see you again, Santi.'

The commander hurried six squares south, four east, and engaged a bespectacled man with healthy black hair that was just a little too dark to be true. Siri looked at the ruddy faced woman beside him and could tell she was about to launch into a dialogue neither really wanted. Siri didn't do small talk. He crouched down to adjust a sandal just as she began to speak. The sound of children distracted him. There was a play area at the far end of the garden with swings and a jungle gym. The children of those unfortunate enough to have them were screaming and being precocious. Like their sophisticated mothers and fathers, they were dressed in their finest clothes and were showing off in a most obnoxious way.

'A coroner?' he heard the woman say above him. 'Fascinating. My sister, Dara recently passed away . . .'

'That wasn't my fault,' Siri said. 'Excuse me.'

He caught up with Khoumki and the treasurer and made a threesome. He'd actually met the treasurer when the man was still teaching mathematics in a cave in Vieng Xai. Siri nodded at him and turned to the well fed face of the commander.

'I believe it was on that campaign in '66 that I pulled a bullet out of your gut and saved your life,' Siri said, smiling. 'If that hasn't earned me a two-minute conversation I can't imagine what would.'

The commander appeared angry at first, annoyed at this blip on his soirée. But then he laughed, put his arm on Siri's shoulder, and said, loud enough for all around him to hear,

'I doubt I ever needed anyone to save my life, Doctor. You see, I had faith, faith in the revolution, faith in the system. That's what got me through every battle, nothing else.'

Siri remembered young Captain Khoumki very well. He'd never seen a soldier with so many Buddha amulets under his shirt. He recalled the night when Khoumki's fever broke and the tearful captain told his surgeon if he needed anything, anything at all, his life was Siri's. Siri had saved the man's future but obviously not his memory.

'But you can have your two minutes, Doctor,' Khoumki consented. He was a big man and Siri decided punching him on the nose would only lead to reciprocal injuries. And, as he'd come so far and waited so long, he decided to make his pitch regardless. The treasurer drifted away once the word 'Hmong' left Siri's lips. And the more he spoke, the more Siri realized he was wasting his time. There's a look, an expression, a man adopts when it's obvious the anti new idea shutter is up. He nods too often and says, 'Aha' even when his eyes are scanning the faces of the guests around him. Once you see that expression you know the man's mind is shut tight as a Tiger Balm jar.

Yet Siri diverted his eyes only once during his allotted two minutes and what he saw made him lose his train of thought completely. He stopped midsentence, abandoned the confused commander, and walked to the edge of the lawn. What he saw removed all hope from his heart. He knew his cause was lost.

18

WEDLOCKED

On the fifteenth of January, 1978, Siri and Madame Daeng were married. It was a two-part affair. In the morning, the bride and groom arrived at the registry office on That Luang and sat on one of three long benches. As motorcycles, marriages, and intentions to transfer cattle ownership or open a smallholding were all registered at the same place, it was necessarily a busy scene. Oil-smudged mechanics sat alongside men and women ripe with the scent of manure, who in turn sat beside couples in their Sunday best. Siri wore a navy blue Mao shirt and sandals. The shirt was freshly laundered but not ironed. Daeng had come straight from the shop but had had the decency to remove her apron before heading out. They had the required paperwork with them. It was several inches thick and in triplicate.

When their turn came they were shown not into a chapel or a private room but to the third desk from the end of a long busy row. Their officiant was in his thirties with the pallor of hepatitis on his skin and a drape of greasy hair that fell across one eye. He didn't bother to look up as they sat on the non-matching chairs in front of him.

'Documents!' he said, tapping his forefinger on the desktop.

It was probably the liver spots on the hand proffering said documents that brought him out of his clerical trance. He looked from Siri's face to Daeng's, then back at Siri's, and grimaced unkindly. He obviously didn't take well to complications.

'Look,' he said. He spoke very carefully and at a volume he hoped the elderly people in front of him would be able to hear. 'The system has changed.'

Daeng grasped Siri's hand and suppressed a laugh.

The man pressed on. 'These days we don't need the parents' – he looked more closely – 'or the grandparents of the betrothed to attend a ceremony. Everything's done through documentation.' He held up a sheet of foolscap. 'That means papers. If the couple is adequately matched and share a philosophy to further the cause of the Republic, then—'

'We aren't—' Siri began.

'If you wish to take photographs with your relatives you can do so outside, granddad. There's an attractive hermaphrodite oak in bloom in front of the building, grandma, that'll look nice in your album. Now, why don't you both—'

'Son, slow down there,' Siri said in a strong, loud voice that caused other officials to look up.

The clerk sighed, 'What?'

Daeng knew what she could expect from her beau in circumstances such as these but this was her day, too. She squeezed Siri's hand and smiled at him before rising from her seat. She walked around the desk and sat on the smallest pile of paperwork at the front corner. The clerk scraped his chair away from her. She leaned into his very personal space and brushed some imaginary lint from his shoulder. Her large black eyes bore into the average brown button ones of her victim. They apparently left him paralyzed.

'Yours,' Daeng said very calmly, 'is a job that does not involve a great deal of thought. You receive the pile of documents. You thumb through them to see if they're all in order and copy the names of the couple onto your list. You read out one or two spurious legal lines from the handbook and pepper them with quotes from Mr Marx or Mr Lenin that have nothing to do with love or happiness. You tell us we must be good servants of the socialist state, get us to sign a certificate, and hand us the smudged back carbon copy to take home.'

She looked back at her smiling bridegroom, then stood and looked down at the clerk.

'Just do your job,' she said. 'Don't make it any more embarrassing than it already is.'

In six minutes it was all done. They didn't fall into one another's arms and kiss and express their joy because what they'd endured was nothing but a bureaucratic exercise to feed the state's hunger for paperwork. Siri returned to the morgue, Daeng to her shop to meet the busy lunch crowd. There would be no evening shift that day as the shop was booked for a very special private function.

Siri and Civilai sat like one creature on the rattan sofa at the back of Madame Daeng's café. Their wrists were encased in thick wads of ceremonial strings like suicide survivors. They had their arms around each other's shoulders and their heads abutted: Siamese twins joined at the brain. They wore matching leis of jasmine and held mugs of actual Western whisky in their free hands. Scotch hits drinkers trained on rice alcohol hard.

'Good show, wasn't it?' slurred Siri.

'The best, little brother.'

'What was your favourite part?'

'Oh, I liked the bit where you dropped the bowl of ornamental flowers on the abbot's foot.'

'I made that part up myself.'

'Well done.'

'It wasn't that heavy.'

'He swore as if it was.'

'Well, he should have been wearing shoes. His fault.'

'How do you feel?'

'About breaking his toe?'

'About being married again.'

'Happy as a loon. I'm the type who needs a woman in his life, old brother. So are you. We're hopeless on our own. The ten years since Boua died have been much longer than the thirty-five we were together. I've been an elephant with only two front legs. I need my rear end with her tail swishing away the flies.'

'I'm sure Daeng will appreciate the analogy.'

'It's a compliment. I find elephant rear ends very attractive. I'm lucky to have her.'

'I agree. But don't forget Xieng Noi.'

'Why do you only quote literature when you're drunk?'

'It's the only time I can remember it. Whisky stimulates the attic of my mind, where all the books are stored.'

'So, what about him?'

'Who?'

'Xieng Noi. I can't begin to not forget him till I know how he's connected to my marriage.'

'Xieng Noi spent the greater part of his early life in the monastery. Then, out of the blue, he was taken by a great desire to have a wife. The passion overwhelmed him until one day it occurred to him he didn't have the wherewithal to hang on to the type of woman he desired. So he gave up his quest and went to work on the land instead.'

'That's it?'

'Yes.'

'So . . . what's it got to do with me?'

'Do you have the wherewithal to keep Madame Daeng?'

'I can't think why not. I'm something of a catch, you know.'

'You won't do her much good in a re-education camp.'

'Why should I . . . ?'

'That one-man demonstration last week. People have been shot for less.'

'How sweet of you to worry about me after all these years.'

'A few more tricks like that and she'll realize what she's let herself in for. She'll get on her bike.'

'I'll let the air out of her tyres.'

'There's no hope. I'm sorry to tell you, senility has finally caught up with you.'

'And you, of all people, should know what that's like.'

'I think those Hmong have bewitched you.'

Siri looked away and Civilai knew there would be no more discussion of the topic that night. Something was troubling his friend but this wasn't the right place to talk of sad things. This was a time for celebration. They stared out at the vaudeville that surrounded them. It was like an Italian film they'd once seen: so many bodies and movement and colour, but no real plot. People from Siri's house were there zooming in and out of focus, and the morgue folk, and Phosy. And there were certainly two little fat babies being handed around like hors d'oeuvres. And, yes, there were monks and a guitar player and a dog or two that had wandered in off the street.

Auntie Bpoo, the transvestite fortune-teller, was dressed in a gold lamé ball gown and army boots. Crazy Rajid, the Indian, had kindly consented to wear clothes for the evening. And of course there was the beautiful Madame Daeng, splendid in her pink costume and her oh-so-subtle make-up. Every time she drifted into view Siri sighed and remembered what a lucky old soul he was.

'You do realize,' Civilai slurred, 'this is all illegal. A religious ceremony and music and fun. Fun is certainly against the constitution.'

'You're right. I shall turn myself in to Judge Haeng first thing in the morning.'

'And where is your saviour tonight? I was sure you'd invite him in thanks for rescuing you from the jungle.'

'I did, but he had an appointment with his publisher. Something about his memoirs: how he single-handedly turned back a thousand Hmong warriors and carried one frail old doctor on his back for a week.'

'I'd buy a copy.'

'Me too.'

'And talking about rescues—'

'You're good at that.'

'What?'

'Linking unrelated topics.'

'Thank you.'

'So . . . ?'

'Eh?'

'Talking about rescues . . .'

'Oh, yes. Your American friends: the dead ones. I keep meaning to ask. Whatever happened to them?'

'Danny and Eric.' Siri recalled the Air America pilots fondly.

They clinked glasses.

'They should be home by now. I took them to the American consulate.'

'It's still there?'

'It's a little more subdued than it used to be but the officials seemed suspiciously glad to see me. I imagine I was the first bone hunter they'd seen who didn't ask for money.'

'Did they give you anything?'

'A ballpoint pen.'

'Life just gets better.'

'Amen.'

Madame Daeng, temporarily freed from the shackles of arthritis by Dr Johnnie Walker, danced a sort of hula in front of her blushing husband.

'I think that woman's making advances toward you,' Civilai said.

'Huh, I'm not that easy.'

'Yes, you are. And talking about loose women . . .' He squinted to make out the familiar shape of his wife through the throng.

'She's over there playing with the twins. You know, we're looking for a wet nurse. I don't suppose . . .'

'Hoo, brother. The contents of those churns evaporated many years ago. But I volunteer to help you conduct the interviews.'

'Is that orange juice in her glass?'

'She doesn't drink when she's driving. Best move I ever made, teaching her the basics of the internal combustion engine. Saved my life on a number of occasions.'

'She obviously prefers a live husband.'

'Yes, I *am* live, aren't I?'

He seemed to ponder that point for a few seconds before reaching over to kiss Siri on the nose.

'If that was a come-on you've chosen entirely the wrong night.'

'It was a thank-you.'

There was no reason for Siri to ask what for. The events surrounding the thwarted August coup had affected them both.

'Are you really OK about it?'

'Your bride and I have been talking it through.'

'And it helps?'

'I'm down to four bottles a night.'

'Counselling's a marvelous thing.'

They drank and smiled and tried to make sense of the colourful blur around them.

'And what about your Hmong?' Civilai asked.

19

COITUS INTERRUPTUS

'And what about your Hmong?' Daeng asked.

Siri was lying on the honeymoon bed watching Daeng slowly unwrap herself from her clothes.

'I don't think this is the appropriate occasion,' Siri decided.

She stopped her striptease.

'Then I'm not showing you any more.'

'Oh, come on. This is our wedding night.'

'Then I want you with me. All of you, mind and body.' She sat on the end of the bed and looked at him. 'Since you came back from the commander's party you've been sad and I want to know why.'

'Oh, Daeng. We're three-quarters drunk. How on earth can we have a serious talk about anything?'

She stood and gathered her wrap from the chair.

'I'll be sleeping in the other room.'

'No! Don't. I've earned this. How many other men do you know of my age who'd agree to abstain before the wedding?'

'I'm serious.'

'All right. All right.' He lay back on the pillow. 'I saw something.'

'What?'

'It won't mean anything to you.'

'Try me.'

He puffed air from his lungs.

'At the house, there was an area for the kids of the guests to play. Something was attracting the attention of most of them. I couldn't see at first what it was but they were fighting over it. I was talking to the commander and I looked over and realized what they were doing. Do you know what a pogo stick is?'

'No.'

'It's a stick with a spring. Kids use it for jumping about like a kangaroo. It's a toy. Until the day the Hmong left, it had been sitting on the shaman's altar in the village in Xiang Khouang.'

'Why?'

'They believed it had brought a curse to their village. They couldn't beat it so they worshipped it. They took it with them when they left. The fact that it was at the commander's house told me the Hmong had been caught. Some arse-licking captain had brought it back from the massacre as a gift for his boss's kids.'

'You're sure it was the same toy?'

'How many pogo sticks can there be in Laos? But, yes, I'm sure. I went to get a closer look. There was still wax on it and traces of spirit money stuck to the stem. There's no doubt in my mind.'

Daeng stretched along the bed and stroked her husband's face.

'Siri, you remember the day you proposed?'

'Of course.'

'You told me about your little spirit problem.'

'Yes?'

'You said you see them, the ghosts of the departed.'

'I didn't think you believed me.'

'It's hardly something you'd make up on the day you most want to impress a girl. No, I believed you.'

'Thank you.'

'So, have you seen them?'

'The Hmong?'

'Yes! Wouldn't they let you know if something had happened to them?'

'It's unpredictable. I never know who'll show up or when. But, no, I haven't seen them.'

'Given what happened there, I'm sure they'd make the effort to contact you, especially that girl of yours.'

Siri blushed. 'What girl?'

'The one you avoid mentioning. The one who gave you the tapestry.'

'Well, why . . . ? There's no reason why she . . .'

'It's all right, my husband. She only stole a little part of your heart. There's plenty left for me. More than I deserve. All I'm saying is that if something did happen to your friends, if they were killed, I believe you'd have some confirmation of it by now.'

'But what about the pogo stick?'

'I think you should assume they discarded it on the journey. I can't imagine why they'd want to take a curse with them in the first place. It wouldn't surprise me if they deliberately left it where the PL soldiers would find it. I bet they wanted to pass on the curse to the other side.'

Siri thought about the commander and the trappings of his new corrupt life. Of all the people who deserved a curse . . .

'You might be right,' he said.

Madame Daeng got to her feet and undid another button.

'I'm always right. Now, where were we?'

Siri smiled. 'I'm not sure I'm in the mood anymore.'

'Oh, Dr Siri Paiboun, sweet, sexy Dr Siri. We'll see about that.'

And one more button eased its way from its slit.